CONSEQUENCES
OF CRIME, GREED, & LOVE

CONSEQUENCES
OF CRIME, GREED, & LOVE

BARBARA MOSTELLA

For permission requests email: Mostella1914@gmail.com.

Visit the author's website at: www.barbaramo08.com

Publisher: Barbara Mostella

Library of Congress Registration Number: TXu 2-249-380

ISBN:978-0-578-87043-4 Paperback

Printed in the United States of America

DEDICATION

This book is dedicated to my husband, James Oliver. Thank you for being so loving and patient with me while writing this book. It was your inspirational words that kept me motivated every day. I can't imagine life without you.

Chapter One

TWO-YEAR PLAN

It wasn't enough for Alphonso's four siblings to tease him about finding a wife, but the bosses at Soco & Soco were doing it, too. They didn't understand that it was difficult for him. In this age of social media, there was a plethora of dating apps and independent women to choose from. He had been running nonstop in the past and didn't have time to find a soulmate. But since he'd finished working on his most recent case and was back at home, he could take time out and make plans.

Alphonso loved snow, and it fell a minimum of sixty-one days from September to April in Alaska. But he woke up this morning to his alarm and a fantastic view of rising sunshine beaming through the curtains after weeks on the road.

He lived at a community catered to singles. At thirty-seven years old, it's time for Alphonso to box up this single life and settle down with his soulmate and children.

His two-year plan to find a soulmate started today on this Monday morning. The first step was putting a calendar on the wall near his bedroom to be visible every day as a reminder.

The second step involved calling Jocelyn and setting up their first date. For the last three years, she'd been the Delta Airlines attendant who'd always did his reservation check-in whenever departing Fairbanks International. She'd flirted with him every time. Sometimes he'd acknowledged her gesture, but he didn't need to give a false impression. He'd often wondered how she was there every time that he flew.

She'd surprised him with a phone call while he was wrapping up a situation in Washington, DC. He'd managed not to give out his contact information to her. But guessed that she'd viewed it from his travel profile with the Airlines—and he suspected that was illegal. It flattered him that she'd go to that extent to connect with him, but on their initial date, he'd intended to ask how she'd retrieved it.

His third step was falling in love, and the timeframe has to be cut short. This was his favorite and perhaps the most challenging rung on the settling down ladder. It meant he had to find his future wife sooner rather than later. Otherwise, it could take longer to find the right person, extending for weeks and months for different reasons. The Soco brothers could put him on a case that took him out of the city for an extended period, or he could meet several women and not be able to decide between them. There was so much to consider.

His fourth step meant looking for housing that his soulmate would have to approve. He saw them living in a four-bedroom house, with an office for two, a large family room, a small formal dining room, a big eat-in kitchen for family time, and a massive backyard to entertain several growing children. He didn't need to move fast with this one because he could find somebody who didn't want children—or maybe just the one. Having an enormous yard might be wasteful in that case.

The smell of coffee drifting through to his bedroom reminded him of being in a Starbucks coffee shop. Alphonso had to shelve his soulmate planning for now and get out of bed, get a shower, and have some breakfast. While finishing up breakfast, he'd searched through emails on his phone and found no updates for the meeting at nine a.m. with the firm. Neither of the brothers had sent him an agenda for the morning meeting. The only information given was that it was a potential new client, and the session wouldn't last longer than an hour.

His employer, the Soco & Soco law firm, was owned by four brothers. Thirty years ago, their father opened the first office at his home in Fairbanks. Since his death, the four brothers had launched new branches in Alaska, Washington, DC, and Atlanta, Georgia. Jason and Jermaine were the two that employed Alphonso.

He loved the firm's family environment, which had kept them in business for a long while. Neither brother decided anything involving the firm without the other's consent. He wouldn't work any place except there, but that could all change if he found a soulmate living outside the state of Alaska.

Alphonso had mentioned to Jason about asking Jocelyn out on a date. He thought Jason would be excited for him, but he was silent and didn't give an opinion. Alphonso wondered if Jocelyn had something on Jason that could damage the firm. His lack of reaction made Alphonso paranoid because he was so out of practice, and dating had not been on his radar for years.

Some would say he was a strategic person, but he disagreed, even though his actions and planning appeared that way. Before going to bed at night, he decided what he would wear for work the following day. If that was being strategic, he could be guilty. It was a habit he'd established over his career. But he was never late for work, and the thought horrified him. His favorite socks are Bombas. They were his good luck charm, and he had several pairs. He gave the same socks to the brothers at Christmas. Maybe some of his luck could rub off on them because they had no clue about current styles in men's fashion, and Alphonso felt he must educate them, even if it was only from toe to calf.

Back in his bedroom, getting dressed, he'd looked at himself in the mirror. Man, he was still in the game and always looked his best because you'd never knew when ladies may be scouting.

He was excited about going into the office because he'd enjoyed his work. It was always exhilarating taking on a new case. Before walking to the garage to get in his navy blue 1947 Mercedes 170 V given to him by his father, he picked up his car keys, briefcase, laptop, and cellphone from the dining room table. It was the first car his father owned, and he hoped to pass it down to one of his children someday. His nieces called it an older man's car, but what did they know? She was a beauty. A classic collector's item assembled in 1936 in Germany, and she was still in good shape. He wasn't sure what value it held, but he would find out when the occasion presented itself. If he followed through with his four-step plan, he and his wife would ride in this car together for Sunday afternoon joy rides. He had to put a step in his stride; otherwise, today would be his first day ever late for work.

Chapter Two

THREAT IS REAL

Monday was Alphonso's favorite day of the week. He saw it as a new beginning to his life after the weekend. Most people dreaded going to work on this day, but not him. His arrival time of 8:45 a.m., five days a week, was the same since being employed by Soco & Soco. He could drive there in his sleep, and anybody watching could predict his arrival.

He had worked as an investigator at the firm for fifteen years, and his tenure gave him certain privileges. One of which was a parking place next to the owners and the administrator. Each time he pulled into his space, he got a sparkle in his eyes and a smile on his face from seeing his name displayed in gold lettering. It gave him a sense of importance to the firm. The parking lot was elaborate, and the building exterior was also breathtaking. They'd constructed it with gray stone and mortar, with lots of windows and high ceilings. It felt like you were walking into a corporate headquarters as you reached the front door entrance.

Getting in the building without greeting Joan, the administrator, in the mornings was impossible because she sat ten feet from the door. She was the first employee to be hired by the brothers; therefore, she knew everybody's business at work and home. But she was the glue that kept the firm running every day. If everyone did what she suggested, their days would go a lot smoother, and she was not frightened to tell them so. Alphonso had been out of the office for several weeks. It gave him a new appreciation of his job. He could rely on Joan to bring him back to reality as soon as he stepped in the front door.

"Good morning, Joan. How is the temperature at Soco & Soco?"

"Right now, it's okay, but that could change any minute. Ask me after the 9 o'clock meeting."

"Are there any urgent messages for the most eligible bachelor in the firm?"

"No, nothing yet, but it's still early. Are the vacation plans completed?"

"Yes, and I can't wait to walk on the beach, lay out in the sun, get a tan, and just relax."

"Is the bachelor going alone?"

"Not sure."

"What does that mean? It seems like you've been holding out on some information that I should be privy to."

"Let's continue this conversation later. I can't be late for the meeting."

"See you there. The bachelor was always running away when there was a serious conversation about human situations and his personal life."

There was just enough time for Alphonso to put his things on his desk and grab a pad. Whenever they interviewed potential clients, he was always the first to arrive, and he liked that. It gave him a few minutes to breathe and think about his day before speaking to anybody except Joan. Jason was the man in charge during meetings and for any potential new business. He did all the introductions and gathering of information.

The conference table in the room was massive and was only used for interviews, office parties, and staff meetings. Alphonso felt the table was something you would expect in a boardroom of fifteen or more people. He supposed when you were rolling in money; you could afford the best. The two brothers came in, interrupting his thoughts.

"You appear to be deep in thought, Alphonso." Jason looked at Jermaine and grinned. As annoying as his precise manner was, Jason was used to his odd ways. His mannerisms were not what made him marketable in his field, but the results he got from every case they assign him.

"No, I was thinking why had we kept this big conference room table, except for its beauty."

"It's coincidental that you mentioned the table. Jermaine and I discussed getting rid of it and putting a smaller one in. We would need to add more furniture because the table takes up most of the room. That's a topic for another day." As soon as he'd finished talking, Joan came in with the client.

To Alphonso's surprise, it was somebody he knew as a teenager in high school. Seeing her again brought back memories. And he was taken aback. He hadn't forgotten many things about her since high school.

Today, she had a soft, smelling fragrance that was just enough, and it was a significant thing about her that he couldn't recall.

She had great work ethics even back then. Her parents owned a business, and she worked long hours every weekend. The students whispered around campus that her parents didn't have a life, so they didn't allow her to have one, either. She missed out on most of the social gatherings that he and their classmates had attended.

He wondered if she had gotten married or had children. Jason interrupted his thoughts with introductions.

"Good morning. For the benefit of our potential client, I will introduce everyone. I am Jason Soco, and this is my brother Jermaine Soco. We are the owners of this branch of Soco & Soco. Alphonso Lott, our lead investigator at this branch, has a team of four working with him. Each of which you will meet later. He and his team are the best you will find in any law firm. You have already met the boss and the CEO of this firm, Joan Hasting." Everybody laughed.

"Seriously, if Joan wasn't here, we'd be off-course. She works harder than all of us put together."

"With us today is Amelia Haley. She is the Co-owner with her brother William Haley and CEO of Hotel International-Anchorage. Welcome, Amelia, and thank you for choosing our firm; at least, after our meeting today, we hope you will choose us to represent you."

"Good morning, and I'm glad to meet each of you."

"Amelia comes to us because she has received several threats from a real estate developer," Jason explained.

"No evidence has surfaced to determine if multiple companies are involved. They want Amelia to sell her hotel and the land it's built on. Then replace it with live work and play townhome community. Amelia, can you give us more details regarding the situation?"

"Thank you, Jason. As most people call it, Hotel International-A has been in my family for over thirty years and has had a five-star rating for most of those years. This rating was given for excellence in 24-hour reception, daily housekeeping, and multilingual staff. For the last ten years, our occupancy rate has been at 80 percent, and sometimes higher depending on the season. The industry puts hotels into types rather than just having standard ratings such as deluxe, first-class, tourist class, and standard. Our hotel is a deluxe luxury."

"Over the past five years, the hotel had a facelift and upgraded to the current standards. My brother wanted me to sell the hotel but did not put any pressure on me. I believe someone might have influenced him. I refused because our parents worked all their lives to make this hotel a successful and profitable business. They left it to us to carry on their legacy. Eventually, he gave up trying to get me to sell. William reaps the benefits of quarterly dividends and had no problems with my management style."

Alphonso's attention had drifted while she was speaking. When she'd walked in with Joan, he noticed she had on an above-knee dress that exposed her beautiful and shapely legs. He had to pull himself back to focus as she continued.

"I can understand why someone would want our hotel. It's in the heart of downtown, where businesses are thriving, shopping options with no state sales tax, and entertainment galore centered on millennials.

We are close to parks, several ski resorts, and the largest museums in the state. Anchorage is the starting point for rails, and anyone can visit beluga whales about 6 miles south. All three species of black, brown, and polar bears are found here.

The cost of living in the area is not expensive, and where else except Anchorage can you get the best reindeer sausage. Our elected officials continue to pass laws and ordinances to assist the local police department deter the increase in crime. But none of this explains why these people are trying to force me to sell, which will never happen."

"Thank you, Amelia. How long have these threats been going on?" asked Jason.

"About three months. I thought by now the police would've figured out who's behind the threats—the first ones were messages to my cell phone from what the police called a burner or prepaid phone. My technical skills are not at the level of these people; so, I couldn't identify their software. The police think the phone is a jailbreaking model that is not traceable. This type of phone has some legal and federal limitations."

"I see," Jason said, making notes.

"After that, I received encrypted email threats. I knew these people had my home address after receiving postal warnings. The police have been doing what they can, but it was time to get legal representation. With not knowing where the criminals were located, I was skeptical about getting help in Anchorage. Therefore, here I am, and that is my reason for the visit today."

"If you have the paper threats that came in the mail, we'll need to see them."

"Yes, I do. I've also saved voicemails and text messages on my phone."

"Alphonso's team will coordinate with you to get those copies when you meet with them. Well done for not deleting anything; many people in your position do."

"Amelia, these clowns know where you live, so is there anywhere else you can stay while the investigation is ongoing?"

"I live in my parent's home in Anchorage and have lived there since they died. However, we have a vacation home in Fairbanks, where I'm staying for a few days before returning to the hotel. It's a seven-hour drive from Fairbanks to the hotel and living in my parents' home is too dangerous. I thought about staying at our holiday home, but I don't feel safe there, even though it's gated. Starting tomorrow, I'll be staying in a hotel guest room until your firm and the police catch these criminals. I need to be around other people."

"That's a great idea and very sensible. We will need the addresses of both of your homes."

"Of course."

"You said, 'until our firm brings these criminals to justice.' I'm hoping that we have satisfied you with what we've discussed and that you will become our client?"

"I did some research before coming here, and I'm impressed with your firm's credentials and the reputation you have in the community. Hopefully, I can afford you." There was laughter throughout the room.

"We are reasonable, and I'm sure you can afford us. A contract will be drafted that lists our fees, and we'll send it electronically by tomorrow for your signature. If you disagree, please call us, and we will make it work for you."

"I like the sound of that."

Jason turned to his colleagues, "Amelia has provided the firm with a copy of the harassment complaint she filed with the Anchorage Police Department. Two officers were assigned to work on this case. They think one or more companies have harassed other businesses in the area similarly and have succeeded. Alphonso and his team will start work immediately on discovery."

"Is your brother aware of what's going on?"

"No. But we haven't communicated in several months. I can handle this without his input. From our discussion today, the fewer people that know, the better."

"We are all in agreement with that."

Alphonso made a mental note that still waters run deep. There was more going on between Amelia and her brother than she'd let on. Her brother was the first person she should want to confide in.

"Amelia, you've done more than most people would under the circumstances. You have given us enough information and documentation to get started, so we'll do our best and work with the Anchorage police to stop these threats of a takeover. We'll come up with a strategy on how best to work the case. As soon as we have any evidence of who is behind these threats, we will contact you with an update. So, for now, that's it. Thank you for taking the time to come to our office and for putting your trust in us."

"We won't let you down. Joan will provide you with relevant contact information. You can give her the addresses of your two residences and the hotel. You are welcome to call anytime. We are on call 24 hours a day."

"Thank you, and I look forward to hearing from you soon."

"Joan, please escort Amelia to Alphonso's team, so they can extract the information from her phone. Ask them to bag the postal mail so that they can work on the technical forensics. Alphonso, I need you to hang around for a few more minutes."

They waited until Joan had escorted Amelia out before Jason spoke again.

"Now that it's just the three of us here, Alphonso, we want you to proceed with your vacation to Florida next week, but we would like you and your team to start on this case before you leave. Let's see if we can get it wrapped up by the time you return or soon after. I believe this case is going to be like no other that we've taken on before. Amelia's brother lives in Pensacola. If you can get an interview with him while you're in the area, it will help solve this case. It would also save the firm from spending additional resources for someone else to travel there."

"I see what you are trying to do. Save a few pennies on travel but spend a lot more on this conference room." The three of them laughed.

"Alphonso, I don't think your calling is a comedian, so why don't you stick to investigating. Putting jokes aside, you might get some historical information about the brother to ensure he is not part of these threats and find out why he wanted to sell the hotel." Jason made notes as he gave Alphonso his instructions.

"I haven't been on vacation in two years, and now you two want me to work this case from the first day of my break."

"Don't get upset. When cases come to the firm, we have to put the best on them, and that's you."

"If you say so. Since I must beat my head on the pavement before getting to enjoy the beach, I'd better start work on the case with my team. I will see you both later."

After the meeting, everybody returned to their offices. While Jason was sitting at his desk, he thought about what Amelia said about the encrypted emails and text messages she received. It came as a shock, and he had pretended to scribble some notes to hide his lack of composure. It seemed a massive coincidence, but he had been getting encrypted threat messages on his cell phone, too. Each one was the same. 'We will reveal your secret. Stay tuned.'

He thought the first one was a hoax and ignored it. But he had received four of the same messages a couple of days apart, and he wondered if it was a genuine threat and where it was coming from. Could it be related to Amelia's case? And should he inform his colleagues?

Chapter Three

SHE SAID YES

The nerve of those brothers wanting him to work while he was on vacation next week is unbelievable. Alphonso wondered how often they worked while they were away with their families.

One thing he couldn't complain about, though, was his office. He'd often complimented the brothers to keep them sweet, but it was another privilege of longevity with this firm. He had a conference room in the corner of his office suite to meet with his team and an extra workspace for when it was needed. His snack area had a microwave, an office-sized refrigerator, and a Keurig K-Supreme coffee brewer. A beautiful window view of the landscape outside made the day go faster. All he was lacking was a comfy bed, and he could live in his office. Who'd ask for more?

He'd wondered what the firm was worth. Having visited their homes, he assumed they were not worried about bills at night when they sat down to have dinner with their families. They paid him and his team well. Their salaries were comparable to industry standards, so they weren't complaining. However, there was no doubt about it; his entire team's salary wouldn't equate to one of theirs.

Before he started the second step of his plan to find a soulmate, which was to call Jocelyn, he emailed his team for a meeting at 1:30 p.m. It was to discuss team strategy for their recent case. For the generous salary he was paid, he had to put in a few hours of work today.

It was 11:30 a.m. Alphonso closed the door to his office, so there'd be no interruptions while he talked to Jocelyn. Her number was fresh in his memory, even though he'd never called it.

"Hello Jocelyn, this is Alphonso your favorite Delta customer."

"Hi Alphonso, such a shock to hear from you. Are you back in town?"

"Yes. In the office doing my normal day-to-day routine. How are you, and is this a good time to talk?"

"Yes. I'm doing great, and your timing is perfect. We've just finished our 11:00 a.m. departure flights and didn't have another one until 3:30 p.m. What could I have done to deserve this special call?"

"Since you put it like that. Would you have dinner with me tomorrow or Wednesday?"

"Yes, I'd love to, but Wednesday would be better. There are some people off sick at work, so I'll be working twelve hours tomorrow to cover their shift."

"Wednesday is good for me as well. Would 6:30 p.m. be a good time to pick you up?"

"Yes. I'd like that."

"One small thing. I need your address."

"I'll text you."

"Are there any food allergies or preferences for dinner?"

"I had a nasty banana allergy when I was younger. I'll spare you the details, but I grew out of it, so whatever you choose will be fine."

"Okay, see you then. Have a great rest of the day."

"Thank you, and you do the same."

Alphonso grinned as he hung up the phone. For a guy looking for his soulmate, that was easier than he'd expected. He felt that no matter what happened for the rest of the day, he could handle it. His excitement was running full speed in anticipation of his date on Wednesday evening. Was that too much excitement for a man his age? No. It was about time.

Since he'd pulled that off for their first date, maybe he'd ask Jocelyn about going on vacation with him next week. That could push his luck.

All that thinking and congratulating himself made him hungry, and he wondered what he'd do for lunch. Then his office phone rang.

"Alphonso, this is Joan. The brothers asked me to pick up lunch for them at Roma's deli. Would you like something, or are you going out?"

"What a coincidence; My stomach was just asking me what we are eating before his team meeting. A sandwich would be excellent."

"It's true what the brothers say. You aren't a comedian."

"Come on, Joan; I thought I'd at least one person in my corner who would come and see me perform at the Comedy Club?"

"Right now, you are 0 for 3."

"Okay. Let's get back to lunch conversation. I will pre-order, and it should be ready when I arrive. It's eleven 11:45 now. I'll return at twelve-thirty."

"A turkey on wheat bread with barbecue chips and a pickle will be great. Thank you, Joan."

"That sounds like a pregnant woman's craving. It's not uncommon for men to have the same symptoms. Is there something you haven't told me? I thought you weren't dating anyone, but here you are having cravings."

"Pickles are something I can eat with every meal."

"If you say so. Lunch is on the brothers. Can you believe it?" Alphonso was not surprised. They did that more often than Joan was aware.

"It's about time they spent some of that cash."

"You know meals are from their expense account."

"I understand that. We must take care of deductions for taxes. Lunch with clients is tax-deductible, even though we are not clients. Are you saying the brothers cheat on their taxes?"

"No, I'm not saying that at all. I wouldn't dare." They both chuckled.

"Thank you, Joan. Will stand by and wait for your return."

"Okay, Alphonso."

He checked his email while waiting for Joan to see if there was any correspondence from the brothers. An email from Jason asked him to estimate the number of hours his team might have to work on this case for Amelia. But he couldn't answer it until the team meeting later. There was an email from Joan to electronically sign for work completed on his last case. He would answer that because he would need that money for vacation next week. It was 12:30 p.m. He'd better wait at Joan's desk for her. Great timing. Joan had just walked into her office.

"You must have smelled the food from your office with that Pinocchio nose, Alphonso."

"This nose could be attributed to my father and I did detect an aroma coming from that direction. My stomach was empty because I only had cereal and coffee for breakfast. Over the past years, I have attributed the stomach to Fairbanks restauranters."

"One of these days, you'll find a wife who will fix you breakfast, but don't expect it all the time."

"Don't you fix breakfast for your family every morning?"

"No, I don't. Two or three times a week if they're lucky."

"Well, I'm working on something romantic as we speak."

"You've given me hints twice today. What is it you're not telling me?"

"No, my lips are sealed, but you, my dear, will be the first to know when and if it happens."

"You have my curiosity up now. Does this lady have a name? Is it someone I know, and is she pregnant?"

"Her name is Jocelyn. She is not pregnant as far as I know, and if she is, even though I am ready for kids, it's certainly nothing to do with me. I don't think you know her. Before you bombard me with more questions, I am more than ready for some lunch. Thank you so much for thinking of me. I don't know what we would do without you in this firm."

"There you go again, getting off the subject and stopping me from grilling you."

"Not at all. I want to eat this food while it's hot. I wouldn't want you to feel that you made the trip three blocks from here to pick up hot food, and then I either let it get cold or don't eat it."

"Okay, I will let you slide this time. Thank you and the brothers for the trust you have in me. Working here is easy because this is my family away from home. I enjoy almost every minute until someone doesn't listen when you know I'm right about something."

"This place is the best, and I have to prepare for the team meeting. Hold my calls this afternoon unless our client Amelia calls, please Joan."

"Will do. What about Jocelyn?"

"Definitely, her."

"Enjoy your lunch."

While he ate his lunch, he couldn't keep his mind off his upcoming dinner date. He knew that since he had mentioned her name more than once, more drilling would come for details from Joan. He suspected there might be some nosey research going on as well. Alphonso just chuckled.

Chapter Four

TEAM STRATEGY

Even though many years and time have gone by, it was great to see Amelia again. Alphonso couldn't imagine how she felt after losing her parents, and now, she had to run the hotel alone. The thugs didn't know what that hotel means to the community. She was in Anchorage, and he in Fairbanks all this time. It was odd that their paths crossed now.

He prepared the agenda and summary for his meeting while waiting for his team to arrive.

His team comprised Liam, Emma, James, and Noah. They had worked together for over ten years. Their unique personalities and skillsets allowed them to work well together. Their familiarity with each other bonded them into a single mindset.

Alphonso didn't mind being out of the office because he knew Liam, his team lead, and the rest of the team didn't need micro-managing and would carry on in his absence. Liam was another cog in this firm that kept it running smoothly. If push came to shove, they could do without him for a few days because of the excellent work Liam did, but he wouldn't tell the brothers they could save money if they fired him. The joke was on them.

His team had excellent working areas, too. Five years before, an office interior design company built professional offices for them, with no expense spared. Compared to what the previous employer gave them, their suites were excellent. Liam and Emma were in one office, Noah and James, in another. Each work area was spacious enough to divide so that the team member could have privacy while working on cases and private meetings when required. In the middle of his thoughts, the team arrived.

"Hello everyone. I hope you had lunch because this will be a two-hour meeting." Alphonso stated.

"Yes, we did because we knew you would be long-winded and would have lots to talk about because you've been out of the office for a while," Liam said.

"I knew I would have to come back and retrain this group starting today. The training is now in session." They all had a good laugh.

"Speaking for the group, we were glad to have helped you solve the case about the native Alaskan family while you were in DC," Liam said.

"I'm grateful for the long hours you devoted to helping with the case. It's a good feeling when we all come together, and a case is solved. We'll do the same with this one."

"Today, the focus is about a threat and harassment case of a hotel owner in Anchorage by an unknown real estate developer. Multiple companies may be involved. They want to build a live, work and play townhome community at the hotel's current location. Hotel International-A is the target. Amelia is CEO, and her brother William is Co-owner. Amelia has filed a complaint with the Anchorage Police Department. This firm is responsible for investigating the incidents and will sue if we find anyone guilty. The police will arrest the criminals for whatever laws they have broken. Our job is to determine the source of the threats."

"I was in James's office when Joan brought Amelia in and introduced us this morning. We got together afterward, and I have a few questions." Liam was the first to jump in.

"Does the brother know how long these threats have been going on?"

"We're not sure about the brother's involvement yet, but he has tried to convince his sister to sell out to some developers. The two of them stopped communicating, and shortly afterward, the threats started. To be clear, we can't rule him out as a suspect."

"What is her marital status and emotional state?"

"None of that came up in the morning meeting. She is still using her parent's last name, Haley. But that means nothing today because many women keep their maiden names after marriage, and some men take the wives' last names. Can anyone explain that to me?"

"It is just a sign of the times right now, Alphonso," Liam said.

"Her parents have been dead for five years, and the hotel has been in their family longer than James has been in the world." They all laughed.

"I have to throw in a punchline every few minutes, so you lady and gentlemen don't go to sleep. You told me you just had lunch."

"We all had a salad because we didn't want to miss your punches," Liam said, laughing with the others.

"Enough fun. Let's get back on track. Amelia has worked at the hotel since she was in high school. One thing we know, she is deeply passionate about the hotel and will not give it up. Whoever is making these threats will have a hard time convincing her to sell."

"Is she living at the hotel?"

"She was living at her parent's home in Anchorage. After receiving threats in the mail, she felt it was safer to move into one of the hotel's guests' rooms. She and William also inherited a vacation home here in Fairbanks, where she has been staying for a few days, and no threats have reached her there yet."

"What kind of security does she have at the hotel and her residences?"

"She has normal security guards at the hotel twenty-four hours a day and cameras in the hallways throughout the hotel and at entry and exit points. The vacation home is gated, but I don't know how secure the regular residence is because it's an older dwelling. And I'm not sure what the police have recommended since Amelia filed her complaint."

"Liam, those were some good questions; they have made me think about other things, like do they have a tracker on her car? Otherwise, how would they know about her parents' home in Anchorage? If so, they know the location of the vacation home. Hopefully, that's something the police have investigated. Someone could have leaked information from insider knowledge from an employee at the hotel. If there are no more questions, I want to make some team assignments."

"Liam and Emma, the first thing I want you to look at is the police report Amelia left with us. First, see if the police checked her car for a tracker and determine the exact date Amelia filed the threat report and what progress has been made. Then look at any companies or hotels purchased or forced out in the State of Alaska over the last five years. If you can, determine whether these companies have any connections or operate in other states."

"You should coordinate with Amelia for a trip to Anchorage to get any other threatening documentation she has. We need to know if any employee is working against the owner for monetary gain or any other reasons such as personal vengeance."

"Is they're already a suspect at the hotel?"

"Not that I'm aware of. Now, all employees are suspects."

"While you're at the hotel, assess the surveillance, security protocols, and any suspicious activity or breach of hotel computers."

"We need to find out who the hotel cyber security lead person is. They would be the ones to answer those questions."

"You are right, Liam."

"James, you already have the phone and email information. You should focus on public records such as pending lawsuits, current and past, entered by any developer headquartered in the State. Look into bankruptcies, too, please."

"Alphonso, I want to know who they purchased the land from? That may not be important for this case but could add to the history."

"James, man, you are on it. That is a great idea. This will be part of Noah's assignment. Elected officials maybe, involved in the sale of that land first purchased by the parents or grandparents of Amelia. The process, how it changed hands. It wouldn't surprise me if Amelia already knows this."

"Noah, I need you to do a search as James has suggested on the sale of that land. You need to investigate real estate companies backed and supported by elected officials. Check with the State for any developer who has renamed their company."

"Everything we do has to be honest and ethical. Keep records of your travel and the hours you spend on this case. Our aim is solving it for the client, and the other important thing is that we get paid." The team responded with a thumbs up.

"I will look at the financial health of the hotel and see if the client has any enemies or past concerns regarding her parents. I'll give the closet a rattle and see if any skeletons fall out. What timeframe do you think we're looking at for this case?"

"We have a fair bit of information to go on, and hopefully, the threats have stopped. It might take two to three weeks, maybe less. It depends on what we uncover from the assignments you have given us." Liam answered for the team.

"That's a good estimate and is in line with what I was thinking."

"You know, my vacation starts Monday next week. The brothers agreed to it before the case came in. Amelia's brother William lives in Pensacola, and I will interview him while I'm there to see if he has any involvement."

"So that's why the brothers approved your time off, so you can kill two birds with one stone, and they will not have to pay for additional travel," Liam said.

"That's the same point I raised with them. It did not impress them. Let's set up another team meeting Friday morning at 11:30 and a meeting with the brothers at 1:00 p.m. I would appreciate knowing how we are progressing before I go on vacation."

"Does anyone from the team have any concerns or need further clarification? Everyone knows what they're doing?"

"We're all good, boss."

"If I don't speak with you before 5 p.m. I will see you Tuesday morning, my usual time."

"Yes, we know you run like clockwork; you will arrive at 8:45 a.m., never later nor earlier."

"I am happy you know my whereabouts at all times."

Everyone laughed. Alphonso and his team returned to their respective areas once the meeting was over. He had an additional concern in the back of his mind afterward, and James had touched on it. Did Amelia's grandparents or parents illegally gain the land in question?

Chapter Five

CLIENT REASSURANCE

Alphonso rarely looked at the landscaping outside his window of the office. When you saw something beautiful every day, eventually, it was familiar and commonplace. He thought about Amelia and noticed how stunning the coreopsis planted around the building was. It's one of the few plants that grow in Alaska. If the plants had an aroma, he thought, it would be like the soft-smelling cologne she had on in the meeting today.

He called to update her and let her know the firm and his team moved forward to resolve her case and gave some comfort. He spent a few minutes wondering if it was creepy and stepping over the mark, giving her a video call instead of using his regular cell. He concluded it was a good thing to do. The lead investigator would want to get a feel for her surroundings. The consultation was a call dripping with professionalism, even if he wanted to see her again. He could tell from the emotion in her voice that she missed her parents very much during their meeting.

He was reminiscing over a conversation he'd had with her in high school and was unsure why he remembered it. It was about family, the closeness of a sibling, and how you depend on them in good times and bad. The relentless pressure parents put on children in their adolescence stage when discovering their sexuality focused on succeeding in their goals in life to carry on legacies in generations to come.

He was trying to determine why there had been a rift in her relationship with William. His push for her to sell out suggested he needed money fast. There was more to it than she was letting on. Either that, or she'd been in the dark, too. Even though she was the eldest and they grew up together, she'd said that he was her protector and the best brother anybody could ask for. He loved hanging out at the hotel growing up, and the swimming pool was his favorite place.

Their dad had always assumed natural progression to the male heir and thought he'd take over the business after he and their mom died. He'd not been fond of hard work for the hotel business. Their focus changed to teaching her about the company because she was interested.

Alphonso could tell that, even now, she was hungry for it with everything that was coming at her. He knew she'd sacrificed her teenage years and spent them working at the hotel rather than hanging out with friends. The hotel was her life, continuing her grandparents' dream was fulfilled, and she's said she had no regrets.

His team had to investigate her past, even though she was the victim. Alphonso intended to dig deep and explore any debts, overdrafts, and mortgages. Still, he felt that she would be as honest as she appeared. Even Jason thought the threats might involve her brother.

William had checked out their parents' will after their death, but there wasn't a clause in it for either of them to buy the other out. They didn't want them to sell the business.

The last time she and Alphonso had met, he was on the debating team in high school. In the cards, he would end up as a lawyer or politician, but he did neither.

The right lady hadn't come along for him all these years partly because he never had enough time to figure it all out until now. But time was ticking on, and he was hopeful of finding her. He had his four-step plan and would have completed the first two after Wednesday evening.

Alphonso bit the bullet and made the call; he could think about it all night and get nowhere, or he could just do it. He clicked the video icon in the corner of his screen.

Amelia was shower damp in sweatpants and was sitting in the vast living room of her parent's vacation home watching TV when a video popped up on her phone.

"Hello."

"Hello Amelia, this is Alphonso. I'm sorry for bothering you in the evening. You sound angry. Is everything okay?"

"Oh, hello, Alphonso. You caught me when I'm looking my worst after getting out of the shower."

"I can't imagine you looking bad, anytime."

"Thanks for the compliment, but I almost didn't recognize the number, so I thought it might be another threat, and if I clicked on the number, they would see my face. I'm glad it was you because I don't get video call requests often, so it threw me for a loop."

"I am sorry and should have texted you to see if it was okay to call. Is this a good time, or shall I call back later?"

"No, no, this is perfect timing. It's good to hear and see you again. It was a big surprise seeing you today. How long have you been at Soco & Soco?"

"I've been working for this firm for fifteen years and will stay as long as they'll have me. They are like my family. It was good to see you as well after all these years. I didn't realize you were still in the area. Listen, I will not belabor, but I called for several reasons."

"Thank you again for choosing Soco and helping to keep me employed. I wanted to get some financial information concerning your hotel. The business must be doing well for somebody else to want to buy it. I'd like to know how you're coping with everything emotionally. All of this must have taken its toll on you."

"I'm feeling better and a little safer than I have in months after talking to your firm."

"I am glad to hear that."

"Do you have any additional security at your vacation home?"

"I have an alarm system and a hired security officer that checks the premises three times a week."

"That's good to know."

"I had a financial meeting with the hotel accountant last week. We're in a powerful position, and I'm thankful for all the people we have working for us and the guests that visit. Our net operating income is great, based on the occupancy rate for the two hundred rooms. I'm going to work tomorrow morning. If you'd text me your email address, I'll have the accountant email our income statement for the last two years."

"Thanks, that information will be helpful to the investigation. You can expect to hear from Liam, who works for me. He'll either be in touch later or early next week."

"Did your brother mention any personal financial problems that could have caused him to get you to sell?"

"No, because he gets a check every month from the hotel dividends that pay all his expenses. But I can't say for sure because we have not had that conversation."

"Amelia, would it be personal if I asked you how your relationship is with your brother?"

"No, I don't mind. Our relationship had been strained for several years. My brother is not a big fan of working and does as little as possible. His being at a distance has not it worse. When this mess is over, I hope we can reach out to each other and be close again. I always looked up to him as my protector when we were growing up. With our parents gone and William in Pensacola, I feel alone most of the time."

"I hope that you can reconnect sooner rather than later."

"Are you aware, or have you seen any suspicious activity from any hotel employees since these threats started?"

"I had no concern before three months ago, but I have been more cautious about everything and everyone."

"We don't want you to feel you can't live your life normally; just keep eyes and ears open."

"I will do that."

"I noticed you are still using the same last name. Are you married or have any children?"

"No, I'm not married and no children; unfortunately, the hotel takes up all my time. After my parents died, I had no time for a social life, not even before, and now all the responsibility is on me. But I made my choices, and I love my career. What about you?"

"I've been busy establishing my career, as well; I'd never married or had any children, either. Anyway, I better not take up any more of your time, and I have a couple of things to finish up before going home this evening. I'll keep in touch, and you be safe. Thank you for everything. If you have any more problems or questions, please contact the police or our office. It was great talking to you and seeing you again, Amelia."
"Goodbye."

"Goodbye, Alphonso."

He'd tried to make her feel safe, and it looked like he accomplished that.

He had not finished his other task, but it was 5:15 p.m. He was out the door and on his way home. It had been a long, busy Monday. But tonight, he'd go home, fix some dinner, find a good movie to watch, go to bed early, and dream about his date with Jocelyn in two days.

Alphonso felt a shiver of excitement jolt through him. He could mark day one on his calendar before going to sleep.

Chapter Six

DATA DISCOVERY

It was unusual to not greet Joan as he walked in the door on Tuesday morning. Jason must have her busy working on another case he expected them to take on. Alphonso had stopped by his neighborhood Starbucks and picked up a coffee for himself and Joan. This was the least he could do since she ensured he had lunch on the brothers yesterday. He put the coffee on her desk, left her a note, and went to his office. She had left several messages on his desk.

One was from Amelia, letting him know she had headed back to Anchorage early that morning. A second one was from Liam, letting him know he would be in at noon. He would give Amelia a call later because he wanted to give her some time to get through the morning traffic. She had a seven-hour drive back to her hotel. It would give him time to check his email and see what was on his schedule for the day.

The workday would be a slow one. After an hour of answering and reading emails, Alphonso looked at the financials of Amelia's hotel that were forward to him from her accountant. Hotel-A was in great financial shape from what he could decipher and not being a financial wizard. He wouldn't expect anything different. Liam had introduced him to a handy software application. It would help him find any background or negative financial information concerning William, Amelia's brother. It appeared he had been doing an excellent job with his financials as well.

He couldn't find any history or financial information about any business William owned in Pensacola.

Alphonso placed a call to Delta Airlines customer service because he wanted to get some information about his profile and how their employees access passenger details. They told him they asked for personal information such as name, address, city, state, and phone number whenever somebody made a reservation. They kept the information on file to prevent identity theft from their customers. When you checked in at a Delta counter, the attendant saw the details. That's why they asked for a photo ID to verify identification. It confirmed for him how Jocelyn had retrieved his phone number. He thought what she did was illegal, but he wasn't mad at her since she had consented to a date with him. He would see how it fell into play to his advantage. It was already 11:30 a.m. Amelia would be halfway to the hotel; he would try to reach her.

"Good Morning Amelia."

"Hello, Alphonso. I recognized your number, and I had a good night's rest last night after talking to you."

"Glad to hear that. I can hear a different tone in your voice this morning, as well. You sound cheerful."

"Your phone call was more than comforting to me and has helped ease my mind about this mess going on. So, I'm going to stay positive."

"That's good news. I received the financials and thank you; everything looks good."

"Were you expecting to find something wrong?"

"No, I was expecting to find what I did. It was just a formality for our investigation. You should have your voucher once you arrive at your hotel if you haven't already."

"I left early this morning and didn't look at any emails before."

"Thank you for letting me know you were getting out early, and I am happy you're feeling better. I am going to let you focus on your driving, and we'll talk soon. Goodbye Amelia"

"Goodbye, Alphonso."

It was such a beautiful day. Alphonso decided he'd go out and pick up Thai food from Lemon, the best restaurant in Fairbanks. He picked up some lunch and food for his dinner that evening. Returning to the office, Joan still wasn't at her desk. What was happening? He hoped she was okay. Checking his emails while eating lunch, he found an office email from Jason, letting everyone know Joan was out that day. She had a family issue and would return tomorrow. That meant it would be even slower without her there. James had sent him an email letting him know he found some revealing information. He'd better call him as he'd finished eating.

"Good afternoon, James. How is your day going?"

"Man, you keep us so busy. I can't get a break."

"I am so glad to hear that Liam is leading by example, except he wasn't coming in until noon today, so I might have to have a talk with him and not his team members." They both laughed.

"What news do you have for me?"

"I was shocked to find out how easy it was to find out bankruptcy information. Amelia's grandparents filed bankruptcy six months before purchasing the land where the hotel sits today. From what I can tell, they paid cash for the land."

"I wonder if Amelia is aware of this?"

"I don't know. The grandparent's only other asset was the old homeplace Amelia's parents left her and William in Anchorage."

"That's some interesting information you have uncovered. Since this home residence is old, it may not have an updated security system. Have you mentioned it to Liam?"

"Yes, I have, and he asked that I make you aware. I'll work on the other assignments you gave me yesterday."

"You are doing an outstanding job, and I don't want to hold you up from going down that path. So, I'll talk to you later."

James didn't report who the land was purchased from. That was going to be an exciting revelation. It was close to going home for the day, and he thought the day would be a slow one. Liam had sent him some preliminary charts to review for tomorrow's update with Jason. He would check them before going home for the evening.

Alphonso was glad that he would not have to fix any dinner when he arrived home that evening because he had picked up his favorite food at lunch. He could mark the second day in search of a soulmate on his calendar. It would be the only exciting thing Alphonso did that evening. He had not noticed earlier, but Amelia had sent a text letting him know she had arrived safely at the hotel. He was glad to hear that, but he didn't text her back. Alphonso didn't want to make her feel like she had to check in with the law firm about her movements.

Chapter Seven

CASE UPDATE

People often say, 'Thank God it's Friday', but Alphonso thanked God for Wednesday morning because tonight was his first date with Jocelyn. His ride into work was filled with excitement and anticipation. He doesn't know how he will concentrate throughout the day.

He'd been working nonstop on Amelia's case for the last two days, and it was a pleasant distraction, but now it was time for some fun. Alphonso has been thinking about what he should wear; he'd wanted to make a good impression. The temperature would be around 40 degrees this evening, so he'd wear his powder-blue sweater and dark blue pants. He laughed at himself, but men are just as fussy as women because they want that first impression to be a lasting one. When searching for a restaurant for their date, the choice was simple. The Chowder House was a local favorite and well known for its varied selections of Chowder, and it was appropriate for the weather. The evening called for a bowl of warming food made from fresh ingredients. First, he had to get through several more hours of work.

Alphonso focused on the final draft of briefing charts developed by Liam and his team. They were ready for his approval and sign-off. The brothers rarely pressured him for results. But they liked frequent updates to see that they were moving forward with the cases. When an assignment came in, it was because somebody was in trouble. They were concerned about every client who went through the door and believed in rapid resolution, even though their bottom line was getting paid. They've understood that we all have bills to pay. If they don't get paid, the staff don't either.

Even though Jason was expecting him, he gave a two-tap knock on the door.

"Come in. Hello Alphonso, how's it going man?"

"Things are great so far. As soon as you're ready for the update on Amelia's case, we can start."

"I'm ready. Let's sit at the conference table, we'll have room to spread the paperwork, and it'll be more comfortable."

Alphonso gave him a copy of the briefing charts. "We've only just started our investigation, so information is limited right now." Explained Alphonso.

"Just give me what you got."

"We'll have more information by Friday. Before we get started, I will say that she's been fiscally responsible, and her parents trained her well. This first slide shows the financial information I've received from Amelia's accountant, and it covers the last two years. The hotel's net operating income is more than we expected. Their yearly occupancy rate handles that. The market value is excellent, and the land pricing is off the chain."

"On Monday, Amelia told us the occupancy rate had been 80 percent yearly for ten years. Is that correct?" Asked Jason.

"Yes, spot on."

"Because of the land value, location, and occupancy rate, it's obvious why a developer is trying to force her to sell."

"The next chart identifies that the hotel is carrying a small loan for construction that included upgrades for the interior and payoff is over one year."

"Good practice, if you don't have to use your capital, take out a small loan," Jason noted.

"As a prequel to my interview with Amelia's brother next week, I've included a summary chart concerning his financials which is none. If there is, he's doing a heck of a job of hiding it. We have not found out if he had any employment or other business at his current location in Florida."

"The following chart data comes from a reliable source. There are multiple companies involved in the threat, and one of them is in Pensacola. Hopefully, by Friday, we will confirm the high-ranking executive's names and start digging to find out who does their dirty work for them. So, I'll be working on vacation by interviewing William and researching our leads on these companies."

"Alphonso, you'll still have enough time to get some sun at the beach."

"I don't see it that way."

"It'll work out, trust me."

"The last chart shows information that surprised all of us. Amelia's grandparents filed bankruptcy before purchasing the land

where they'd hoped to build a hotel. We are still working on this lead to see what other surprises we find."

"This is really a surprise."

"I have a real estate friend that lives in Fairbanks. According to him, one of the leading developers in the area was Robert of RTK, LLC, who died five years ago. His son, whose name he didn't know, became CEO after his death, and nothing but shady deals have gone down with the company since. However, that's the extent of his knowledge, so it's worth looking into. This may be the company you mentioned that's located in Florida. Did James get any information from Amelia's phone that will help the case?"

"He's having a problem. Whoever sent the encrypted text messages is using unfamiliar software. He does the decrypting himself, but this one had him stumped, so he's pulling in some of his technical friends who work for the State of Alaska. As soon as we have something, I'll let you know."

"The messages are key information." Jason had a puzzled look on his face because this particular issue affected him.

"You may be right."

"This is all I have for now. We'll see how far we've got by our next meeting on Friday."

"Friday is perfect."

"Have you been in touch with the Delta attendant?"

"You mean Jocelyn."

"Yes, Alphonso."

"Why would you reference Jocelyn that way as though there's something bad about working for Delta?"

"Darn, you're touchy today. I meant nothing by my remarks. You act like you are married already, and you haven't even been on your first date yet."

"Jocelyn and I have a dinner date tonight, and I am excited." Jason went quiet for a moment.

"Be careful. You never know what plan these ladies you meet at the airport have. Try a dating app."

"There you go, again. I thought you'd be happy knowing I'm dating."

"I am. You have not been on the dating scene for a while. I just wanted you to be careful."

"I could say the same about you. Being married for 25 years does not make you an expert. Do you know something about Jocelyn that you aren't telling me?"

"Why would you ask that? Of course not. But you are right about me, I know little about how dating is today, and I'm happily married."

"I would like to find someone I can grow old with and sit back and enjoy the grandchildren together, just like you."

"My oldest is just turning eighteen and getting ready for college. I don't think I am prepared for grandchildren yet, but I'm sure my wife is. I hope you and Jocelyn have a nice evening."

"I'm leaving at 3 p.m. My date is at 6:30, but I have a few things to do before leaving."

"Okay, Alphonso. It seems like you are heading in the right direction with the case. Let Joan know you're taking off early. She'll have lots of questions about your date."

"Yes, you're right."

"Will you inform Jermaine about the updates and the meeting on Friday? You know he forgets things sometimes, so have Joan put it on his calendar."

"I was joking with him over the weekend about replacing him. Guess what he said to me? I can't do anything without him, and he is partially right. I would have a problem without him and you. Don't let that go to your head." They both laughed.

"I'll see you tomorrow."

Alphonso was overly concerned after he left Jason's office but tried to be as calm as he could be. Jason knew how to get under his skin when he'd wanted to and thought nothing of it.

Alphonso was sure Jason was excited to know he was dating someone, but just not Jocelyn. When he'd told him about this date with her that evening, Jason was speechless for a moment and had a look of disappointment on his face. He was probably hoping the relationship didn't develop into anything and that Alphonso would move on to someone else. He'd even suggested Alphonso go on a dating website and find someone. He still wanted to do it the old fashion way and in person.

Jason and Jermaine were like brothers to him, and he'd trust their judgment on most things.

As a known lawyer in Fairbanks, Jason knew many people and had lots of friends in every corner. If there was something in his way, he'd remove the threat. Alphonso thought Jason was trying to warn him. Having known him all those years, and when Jason sounded an alarm, it was always worth paying attention to. His brother Jermaine was forthright, and if he knew something, he would tell him right away. Maybe after tonight, he'd learn more about Jocelyn and be in a better position to make up his own mind.

Alphonso stopped at Joan's desks to tell her about his early departure and asked about Amelia's calls. If any came through, she should direct them to Liam. How thankful he was she did not give him the third degree. Because he was not in the mood for her today, either, but he was glad to see her back at work.

Back at his desk after shaking off the Jason drama, Alphonso dialed Liam's number.

"Hello, Liam. How are things going this afternoon?"

"Everything great, boss."

"The meeting with the brothers is set for Friday, and Jason was pleased with the update. Is there anything new?"

"James has spoken with the Anchorage Police Department to see where they are with the investigation. They'd checked Amelia's car to ensure there was no tracker on it, and she had alarm systems at both residences. They think it may be an inside job. The report that Amelia filed was recorded a day later, and we don't know why, since the normal practice is to fill the paperwork the same day the incident happened."

"Include this information in the briefing for Friday and anything else that comes up after today."

"Will do."

"See you in the morning, and don't forget, I'm leaving at 3 p.m.

today."

"Okay. Have a good evening."

"I plan on it."

After he'd hung up the call with Liam, he cleared his desk and headed for the parking lot to get ready for his date.

Chapter Eight

JOCELYN'S STORY

It was Wednesday afternoon, and everything was going great for Alphonso, even the traffic. It usually took him thirty minutes to drive home, but today there's less traffic, so he had arrived home ten minutes early. He'd three hours before his date with Jocelyn. He'd walked to his bedroom and, from his closet, retrieved his outfit for the evening. And then he'd washed the strains of his workday away in a ten-minute shower.

Depending on what happened tonight, he may not be going on vacation alone. He'd logged in to his Delta account to ensure everything was okay with his reservation to Pensacola. He'd wait until Sunday evening to do the online check-in for luggage. While logged in, he killed time by checking his social media account. Until tonight, he'd nothing to post.

He's nervous about what to say and how to approach Jocelyn. Because he hadn't dated in a long time. Even though he's seen her regularly at the airport for check-in, this was different. Once dressed and on his way to her house, he'd feel more relaxed.

He should've had a glass of wine to relax before leaving, but he didn't want to meet Jocelyn with the smell of alcohol on his breath. She might even kiss him on their first date. He figured that was dreaming, though. It's a frigid night and a lot colder than he'd expected. He thought the cold might freeze his nervousness and laughed to himself—what a stupid thought.

He'd been driving for twenty-five minutes and listened to his favorite jazz station on the radio. In ten minutes, he'd arrive at Jocelyn's house. Once he got to her street, he'd realized it was a cash-rich neighborhood. He'd wondered how a flight attendant could afford to live there, because they were Beverly-hills housewives type homes. After finding her address, he parked in the driveway. Alphonso rang the doorbell, and It was as though she was behind the door, waiting for him, because Jocelyn opened it right away.

"Hello, Alphonso."

"Hi." He's nervous again, and that's all he could say.

"It's freezing outside. I almost called and canceled, but I've been looking forward to it since you called," Jocelyn said.

"Yes, it is icy-cold."

"Come in, have a seat, and let's get you warmed up before we go out for dinner."

"You've a beautiful home, and I'm so cold that I'd almost forgot to tell you how beautiful you look."

"Thank you, but the house isn't mine. This's my mother's home, and I live with her. She's a retired realtor and has remodeled the house herself. Not to brag, but I'm proud of her. Before retiring, she ran a multimillion-dollar business and had five employees. However, she'd had enough after my father died, so she sold the business. I would introduce you, but she's at a movie."

"Remodeling not something I'd be good at, but your mother was spot on from what I can see. I'm warm enough now if you're ready for dinner."

"Thank you. Let me just get my coat."

As she walked down the hallway, his first question came to mind, why this beautiful woman wasn't married and had no children? Alphonso hoped she didn't notice how nervous he was because he'd wanted to appear sophisticated, not a bumbling wreck. His second question would be, why did she live with her mother? He'd pictured her as the independent type. It showed how wrong people can be in their assumptions—even Alphonso, and it was his job to read people.

Now back outside with both bundled up. Alphonso opened the car door for her, and she seemed impressed, even though he'd trembled in the cold to shut the door for her.

"I believe the temperature has dropped even more. But don't worry, the restaurant is only a few minutes away."

"Where are we going?"

"I thought this would be an ideal night for The Chowder House, as it's such a frosty evening."

"That's a great place. Thank you for being so thoughtful. Even though we live so close to it, I've only been there once, but I've heard people at work say it is their favorite place to go, especially on a cold night."

"I'm glad you approve. It's a good comfort food restaurant. Are you from Fairbanks?" Alphonso asked.

"Yes. I am. What about you?"

"Yes, I'm a native. I travel a lot, but I love it here and I'd recommend this city to anyone. After finishing college, I'd thought about leaving and starting a life someplace else. But things happened concerning my parents. I landed a good job with a law firm. But I'd found out later they were cheating their clients out of their fortunes. Then I saw an opening for a position at Soco & Soco. I've been there ever since and haven't thought about leaving. What about you?"

"I've dreamt of living in Hawaii and going to the beaches every day for some time now. A while ago, I could've transferred with Delta to Daniel K. Inouye International Airport and wouldn't have lost my seniority. But I'd had a few life changing moments that kept me from fulfilling my dreams, as well. How'd you like being an investigator?"

"I don't recall mentioning the work I do."

"You must've mentioned it at the airport during a check in. I'm sure you told me you work for Soco & Soco and what you do for them."

Alphonso was equally sure that he hadn't. Because of the delicate nature of his investigations, he wasn't in the habit of discussing his cases with people. "I think you must be mistaken."

"Oh, well, I'm not sure then. When Delta's passenger's check-in, their profile sometimes shows on our screens. Maybe that's how I came about the information. I hear Soco is the best law firm in the area."

Alphonso paused. She'd thrown him a curve ball, and he didn't catch it. Jocelyn knew too much personal information about him and his employer. Did she know Jason? He'd let her think that he's unconcerned, but he intended to find out what else she knew about him.

"It's a great firm, like working for your family. That's a shorter ride than expected. We're at the restaurant and It looked like others had the same idea, because it's crowded this evening."

He'd made a reservation for two at seven, so they would be okay. It would've been nice if the restaurant had valet parking, then Alphonso wouldn't had to spend time parking his car after walking Jocelyn to restaurant front door.

"If you'd wait for me inside, I'll park the car and be right with you."

"Thank you."

There isn't much privacy for first date discussion in the restaurant, but one thing he knew the food was excellent.

"Will this table be okay, Jocelyn?"

"Yes, this is perfect."

The hostess handed them their menus and told them somebody would be with them shortly.

"I'm not sure what I want. Since you've been here more recent, why don't you suggest something?" Jocelyn asked.

"I've had the Halibut Corn Chowder, with a chicken salad on a croissant several times, and that's what I'll have this evening with coffee. You'd enjoy it."

"That sounds great; I'll have the same, please."

The server took their order and brought their drinks.

"Anything interesting happened at Delta this week?" Alphonso asked.

"We've had more than usual number travelers for every flight, and It's meant working longer hours. A strain of flu had been running amuck among the flight crew, which caused many to work double shifts back-to-back. Tonight, is perfect, I needed the break, and I'm glad you asked me to have dinner with you. What about you?"

"I'll be gone on vacation next week after two years of working flat out. Just making sure nothing is left undone had been somewhat hectic for me." Confidentiality and government guidelines prevented him from talking about his work anyway, but he was careful what he told her.

"Where are you going?"

"Pensacola, Florida for a week at the beach, nothing but fun, and late nights."

"I'm on vacation next week, myself, and I'm jealous."

"Well, here's a radical idea. You could come with me, no strings attached."

"Really, how would that work, seeing as we're on our first date?"

"That would depend on you. An all-expense paid fun trip on Alphonso. We'd have separate rooms at the hotel. One kick though. Since you're employed at Delta, we'd be able to get a discount ticket for you. Am I in the ballpark yet?" They both laughed.

"You would take me with you, even though you don't know me that well."

"In a heartbeat and I can't say that I don't know you because every time I fly out of Fairbanks, I'd go through your agent counter. So technically, we've known each other for several years. I think that makes us safe, don't you?"

"Since you've put it that way, we do know each other. Will tomorrow be okay to give you an answer?"

"Yes, that will be great."

The server brought their food and refilled their cups.

"The food looked wonderful," Jocelyn said.

"As soon as you've had the first bite, you will find it tastes good as well."

"We've gotten to see the sun setting by sitting at the window. Something I've hadn't seen in a while working twelve-hour days. You were right this food is kicking it. These were great suggestions and quite tasty." Jocelyn complemented.

"Glad you're satisfied with my menu suggestions. If there'd be just one thing I don't like about Alaska, it's those times when it's dark all day. If you'll come on this trip with me, will have sunny days every day and none of this Alaska twenty-four hours of darkness," Alphonso emphasized.

"Let's not move too fast. I haven't decided yet. I'd need to take care of something before I can give you a definite yes. I'll call you tomorrow."

"We've had this body warming food but unfortunately, there's no escaping it, we'll have to get back out in the cold again."

"You know, even though we've talk about the dark days in Alaska and the beaches in Hawaii and Pensacola, I do like the cold," Jocelyn confessed.

"Jocelyn, forgive me, I didn't think to ask if you'd wanted any dessert. I told you I was rusty at all this."

"No, I didn't want any. The soup and sandwich were more than enough. I'm going to check out the restroom before we leave."

"Okay, take your time."

He'd hoped she could come on vacation with him. Now that they'd talked, he wasn't as nervous.

"If you're ready, I'll get the car and pick you up at the front door."

"Okay."

"I enjoyed dinner with you this evening, and hopefully, we can do it again."

"It was a pleasure. And it won't be as cold next time. How's it living with your mother?"

"Her name is Ava. We've always had a good relationship and respect each other's privacy. Her home is large enough to have our own space and don't get on each other's nerves. We've our moments, as all children and parents do, no matter what age they are."

"That is great. Do you have any brothers or sisters?"

"No, she and my dad thought I was a handful, and they couldn't handle another one like me. How about your parents?"

"Both of mine live in Fairbanks, in the home where I'd grew up, and we still have a great relationship. I've four siblings, and I'm the only one not married. My nieces gave me a nickname older man."

"You don't have appearance of an old man."

"I'm disappointed. That was a quick drive from the restaurant back to your house. I was enjoying the conversation with you."

He'd opened the door and walked her to the front door.

"Thank you for a great evening. I know it's cold, so I'll let you get back to your car. Have a safe trip home."

"You have a good night, and I'll await your call tomorrow." "Goodnight."

"Good night, Alphonso."

Back on the highway home, he realized it was only nine p.m. She could've invited him in because she'd said her mother was at the movies. He's rattled but felt that dinner went well, and they'd appeared to get along. Alphonso enjoyed her company, and he'd more questions to ask her.

It would take about forty-five minutes to get back home. Alphonso wasn't happy that she knew more about him than he'd knew about her. But she'd said they'd have another date, and she may go on vacation with him. Her lifestyle and living with her mother surprised him. There's nothing wrong with that but, he'd felt that something was off, but Alphonso couldn't put his finger on it. However, overall, it was a good evening that had ended too soon.

Chapter Nine

PLANS AND GRATITUDE

Jocelyn went upstairs to her suite after the date with Alphonso. She'd showered, put on pajamas, and waited for her mother, Ava, and her daughter, Mia, to get home from the movies.

She reflected on the date with Alphonso. She'd hoped he hadn't been suspicious about her knowing he's an investigator at Soco & Soco. She'd slipped up and would have to be more careful. The firm he worked for was one of the wealthiest in the state. She wondered what Jason would think about her and Alphonso going on vacation together. Alphonso had worked at the firm a long time. There's a chance he could know about her deceased husband, Kenai, and the circumstances of his death. She'd guessed if he had, he wouldn't have called her for a date.

She wanted to go on vacation with Alphonso, but she'd have to ask her mother to look after Mia again. No way was she going to turn down an all-expenses-paid trip offer from a first date. If he'd gave her that after a first date, what would he do after the magical third?

Alphonso was a great guy, and she had a good time, but he wasn't someone she would consider marrying. But anything can happen. She knew more about him than she'd let on. The lawyers at his place of employment weren't as great as he thinks, especially Jason. True enough, he's a man that would protect his family no matter the consequences, but she knew his dirty secrets. Alphonso was a way for her to get more information from them Soco brothers first, then get to Hawaii, and hopefully not get hurt.

It's Wednesday evening at ten p.m. Her mother and Mia should have been home by now. However, they were having pizza after the movie, and she'd thought they might be late. Her mother was an outstanding grandmother, and she was always there when they needed her. If it was up to her mother, Jocelyn would have three or four kids.

Mia was the love of my life, and she's enough for me, Jocelyn thought. She'd wished her father knew what a smart, loving daughter she was, but there was an agreement made, and she must stick to it. Otherwise, there would be consequences that wouldn't fall in her favor.

Sometimes she'd wondered if her mother was missing her father more than she pretended. She and her father were married for forty years.

Jocelyn and her father were inseparable. She was an only child and a daddy's girl who couldn't do no wrong. According to her father, no man was good enough for her. He'd disapproved of her marriage to Kenai, even though he walked her down the aisle on her wedding day. After being married for a few years, he grew to like Kenai, which made their marriage better. The relationship with her father was close again.

She'd became unhappy and hid it from her father when the marriage soured, and she realized how rotten Kenai was. She couldn't face the words coming from her mother, 'I told you so,' or her father's disappointment. She was married but had a couple of affairs that her mother knew about. Her father wouldn't have approved. It was during that challenging time in her marriage that Mia was born. She's the love of Jocelyn's life, just as she'd been with her father, but it didn't improve her relationship with Kenai.

Her husband died soon after her father. There was a trial regarding her husband's death, and she didn't think she would get through it. In the end, they ruled his death while hunting in the wood's accidental. Mia was eight months old when he died, so she had no memory of him. Jocelyn couldn't afford the house they lived in after his death, so she sold it and moved in with her mother. Her focus was on the future. Jocelyn was going on an all-expenses-paid trip with a guy she'd only been out with once. Her mother wouldn't react well to the news. The last time she'd warned her about a man, Jocelyn almost went to jail, so her opinion would be interesting.

She heard the front door open and some noise downstairs. She knew it was her Mother and Mia and went to greet them.

"Good evening, Mother. Look like you survived it."

"I enjoy the time I spend with my granddaughter, and I am so happy that I'm retired and can have more time with her. You've done an outstanding job raising her without her father around."

"Without your help, I couldn't have done it, Mother. I need to talk to you. I'll take Mia up for a bath, so she can get to bed because she allowed grandma to keep her out past her bedtime."

"But Mom, we had a good time, and I wish we could've stayed longer," Mia said.

"You're only six, not old enough to make your own decisions, and you have to be in school tomorrow. So, young lady, you march right up those stairs and get ready for bed."

Like most children, she stomped up the stairs and didn't get ready for bed. But when the following day came, it would be a struggle to get her up.

"I am right behind you, Mia, and you don't have to stomp to go up the stairs."

"Okay, Mom."

"That's better.".

After putting Mia to bed, Jocelyn and her mother had a glass of wine in the kitchen. She told her about the plans to go on vacation with Alphonso next week, and she asked her mother to babysit Mia while she was away. Of course, Ava said yes. Her mother asked lots of questions. She'd wanted to know why Jocelyn would go on vacation with someone after a first date, especially with a guy who works at Soco & Soco. Her mother reminded her of all the past failed relationships she'd had and said it was time she got into a permanent one. Jocelyn thought she would feel different, knowing that Alphonso was a native Alaskan, born and raised in Fairbanks.

Jocelyn felt like her mother was always suspicious of anyone she'd dated and worried about Mia. But her mother let her know it was her she was worried about, not her granddaughter. She'd told her mother that it was an all-expense paid trip and who could turn that down. Her mother reminded Jocelyn that money seemed to be the driving force for whatever she wanted out of life, and she's heading down another wrong path. They both said their goodnights and went to bed. Her mother didn't know she'd one more surprise.

Chapter Ten

THREAT GONE TOO FAR

On Thursday morning, driving into work, the anticipation of a call from Jocelyn was driving Alphonso nuts. After last night's dinner, he could move forward with a relationship with her. Overall, he's happier than yesterday. Walking through the firm's front door, he struck up a conversation with Joan as he usually did, but he'd better be ready for questions.

With a big smile from ear to ear, he greeted Joan. "Good morning to the CEO of Soco & Soco."

"Oh. We have jokes this morning. Good morning to you, too. There is a glow about you today, and you left work early yesterday. Do you have something to confess?"

"Actually, there is. I went on a date with Jocelyn last night, and it went well."

"Come on, don't leave me hanging. Give me the details?"

"I can't right now because it's only been one dinner date, and there's not much to tell, but stay tuned to Alphonso 90.1."

"Are you saying it's not a relationship yet?"

"No, not yet. And, I have a busy two days before I go on vacation on Monday, so I'd better get to it."

"Is she going on vacation with you?"

"Maybe. If I get a phone call from a certain female name Jocelyn this morning, I will know more.”

“That sounds serious.”

“Not really. It is better to go on vacation with a companion rather than going alone. Don’t you go reading too much into it, Mrs. Cupid?”

“I hope it works out for you, Alphonso.”

“Talk to you later, Joan.”

“Okay. I left two messages on your desk this morning, and they were both from females, and if I recall, one was from Jocelyn.” Alphonso ran to his desk.

He tried hard to be a nice guy. Joan was right, he’d deserved to be happy, and he hoped Jocelyn was the one.

Joan had left several messages on his desk, both yesterday and this morning. Two were from Amelia and one from Jocelyn.

Something else may have happened with Amelia concerning the threats. Hopefully, the call from Jocelyn was a message saying that she could go away with him. It wasn’t nine o’clock yet, and although it killed him, it was still too early to be returning calls from a law firm.

He’d checked his emails first and would answer his phone messages later. Included in the list of new emails was one from Amelia and one from Liam. Liam had prepared the briefing charts for their meeting on Friday. There were a couple of emails from Jason that he should answer about some upcoming cases, but he skimmed through them and forwarded them to Liam to deal with. Liam was on it and recommending him for employment was one of the best things Alphonso had done. He’s a great buffer to take the pressure off when Alphonso was snowed under.

As they’d grown as a company, Alphonso found the skill of delegation invaluable. Whenever he’s away from the office, Liam took care of things. He knew he didn’t have to worry about things piling up or being left unattended. Alphonso answered his emails and looked at the time. Now he’d call Jocelyn and Amelia in that order.

"Hello, Alphonso. How are you this morning?"

"I am doing great and, how are you?"

"Doing well. Is it too late to say yes to the vacation?"

"No."

"I see we have assigned you to seat 3B first class. Therefore, I need to get seat 3A? We are flying first class, the best way to travel with Delta. I will do my best to shuffle people around if I have to, to make sure I get seat 3A."

"Call me back when you have confirmation, and I'll chat with my trusted credit card to reserve it."

"Okay. I'll call you soon. I have a long line of customers and must go. Goodbye."

Alphonso didn't expect undying gratitude, but it crossed his mind that a bit of thank you might have been in order. He'd put the uncharitable thought behind him and looked at the positives. This was going to be a wonderful vacation. He picked up the phone to get his mind back into work mode.

"Hello, Hotel International-Anchorage, this is Amelia; how can I help you?"

"Hi Amelia, it's Alphonso."

"It is good to hear from you. I tried to reach you several times yesterday, but I got Liam instead. He and Emma are on their way and will be here at 2 p.m., and the police should be here shortly as well."

"What happened?" The reprimand in her voice for not being there for her when he'd said he would, didn't escape him.

"I've had another threat. This time, it came in an eight by eleven envelope that is sitting on my desk. Someone had glued this message onto a sheet of paper, all in individual capital letters. It said, 'I will kill you if you don't sell.' It's more serious than the other threats. My hotel security is with me, waiting for the police to arrive. I believe this is the work of someone who works for me. Only a few people have keys to my office. So, I'm going to change the lock, hire additional security, and ask the police to set up twenty-four-hour surveillance at the hotel."

"Amelia, I'm sorry I wasn't there to answer your calls. But I'm glad you are safe. I know you have my office cell, but I'm giving you my personal cell so that this can't happen again. You're right about around-the-clock security. Please stay with your hotel security until the police arrive. It will be a while before Liam and Emma get there, but I'll call Liam, and he can give me an update once on site. Do you have security cameras that monitor your office?"

"No, only the ones in the hallway that parallels my office. After this, though, I'll be getting cameras inside."

"I'm sure the police will do a thorough sweep of the hotel to find clues about who delivered the envelope. I'll call you later today. What I would suggest is that you don't announce that you're increasing security in your office. We can provide you with some covert cameras in the interim until we solve the case. I'll have Liam pick them up while they are in the area. They are easy to install, and you will have them today. Again, I'm sorry this happened to you."

"What bothers me most is that my grandfather and grandmother worked hard to purchase this land. Their dream was to build a hotel, but at the time, they didn't have the resources. Their vision inspired my parents, who constructed Hotel International-A in their honor. No way am I going to allow these thugs to take away our heritage from my brother and me.

"Amelia, I understand; let's catch these animals before they do any more harm."

"Thank you for calling and being concerned, Alphonso. Goodbye."

Alphonso should've been there as her old friend to comfort her because she sounded sad and afraid. They had to solve this case before anybody got hurt. Alphonso placed a call to Jason and gave him updates concerning the threat. While on the phone, Jason told him about another bribery case that Jermaine was doing the paperwork to determine if it was a case they wanted to tackle. He'd tried to bring his date with Jocelyn into the conversation, but Alphonso put a stop to it and told him there was no need for them to discuss who he dated.

Alphonso believed the answer to this case lay in Pensacola.

His cell phone beeped with a text from Jocelyn. She'd left the information he'd needed to pay for her flight. He had an irritating doubt in the back of his mind saying he's not doing the right thing. Still, instead of paying attention to it, he'd went online and made the reservation for her. She would sit next to him. He logged into the hotel reservation site and booked an additional room for her. Now the vacation was real, and he'd finish up his projects and deadlines. After hours of working on notable cases, he'd felt Liam and Emma should be in Anchorage, and he touched base with them.

"Hello Liam, this is Alphonso. How are things going there, and do you have an update?"

"Yes, I have you on speaker with Emma. We are at Hotel International-A. Officers Connor Wynn and Layla Strong from the police department are here. They've done a preliminary search of Amelia's office and some other areas throughout the hotel with their forensic team. There were no fingerprints on the letter, but there are multiple prints on the door handle going into her office."

"The hallway cameras captured people who have normal access to her office going in and out, and everyone had been questioned. One person is on the suspicious list and is at the Anchorage Police Department for additional questioning. For the next thirty days, a police presence is being provided for the hotel. We looked at the computers with the police and the hotel Cyber team, and no unauthorized access has occurred. The threatening emails we viewed from her phone and laptop were from an internet protocol address that hadn't been identified. We've given the information to James for analysis."

"That's great, Liam. Good work. While you are there, I need you to pick up some convert cameras for her office. The firm has authorized the purchase of them, and you can install them before returning to Fairbanks."

"Only inform essential personnel like the hotel security and computer technicians about the cameras."

"Will do. The officers revealed they have evidence of several real estate companies forcing two other businesses to sell in California and New York. They don't know if they are related to this case. The only difference is that, with the other companies, they didn't threaten anyone's life."

"All this is excellent information that helps our case."

"I don't want to speak out of turn about the police, but Officer Connor Wynn did something that seemed odd. He'd requested a private room to talk to the hotel employee they arrested while we were here with the other officer. Officer Layla should've been in the interviewing room. We will find out why he specified that. We plan to stay overnight at the hotel and leave for Fairbanks early in the morning. I sent you the briefing slides in an email because we won't make the meeting tomorrow morning. However, we should be back in time to attend the one with the brothers in the afternoon."

"Don't worry about either meeting tomorrow. Whatever updates you gather this evening, make sure James and Noah update the charts."

"We'll see you both tomorrow."

"Will do. Goodbye, Alphonso."

"Goodbye."

Alphonso still had Amelia on his mind after talking to her and Liam.

He'd wondered if he had really gotten over her. There were too many unanswered questions.

He shouldn't have Amelia on his mind and be going on vacation with Jocelyn. Time was a cruel master. He'd gone from having zero women of interest in his life to having one too many. He'd pushed his feelings for Amelia aside and finished his tasks. It was five-thirty p.m. and time to go home. He shut down his laptop, locked the door, and left.

Chapter Eleven

IT IS TIME

Jocelyn worked late that Thursday evening and had two hours before going home. She's in the Delta Airlines break room with some friends having a snack. She was tempted to break her good news to them about her plans for a management job in Hawaii with the same airline. But the way they complained about their current positions, she didn't want to add to their unhappiness. Her phone vibrated because she'd turned down the volume. It looked like Tyler; she had tried to call him earlier.

"Hello."

"Hello, Jocelyn."

"Oh, hi, Tyler."

"Did I interrupt something? You sound weird."

"No. I was just taking a break with some co-workers, and it's not often that I get a phone call from my loving and caring brother-in-law."

"Cut the crap, Jocelyn. I didn't call to chit chat. I was returning your call."

"Hold your horses Tyler, I am walking outside the break room so we can have privacy."

"What's going on?" Jocelyn asked.

"You tell me. The last conversation we had, you were coordinating an incident with your friend."

"He's completed the last task we discussed. It turns out that it didn't go smoothly because he was taken in for questioning by the police. I've been informed by other sources that the police are all over the hotel looking for clues."

"Can't I trust you to do anything right? Maybe I'll work with someone else who's more reliable. Do you think your friend will cave in and talk?"

"No, because he knows his family might be in danger if he does. Let's wait this out and see what we need to do next."

"Okay. You know how important the success of this mission is to me. I'm counting on you. How is my niece, Mia?"

"Growing up and looking more like her father every day."

"Are you sure about that?" Tyler asked.

"What do you mean, am I sure? Of course, I know who my daughter's father is."

"Well, you know more than me, then."

"I'd hope so. You weren't there."

"I know you were not faithful to my brother. Even though you weren't getting along, I disapproved of what you did to him. I don't think you know who Mia's father is because Kenai didn't get a DNA test done before he died? And you're no better than he was, always asking me for money."

"You'd throw that one in my face. When we get out of this hole in Fairbanks and are living in Hawaii, I don't want to deal with any of Kenai's family again, especially you."

"I say good riddance to you, as well, as long as you carry out your end of this deal. You won't ever have to see or hear from me again."

"You never cared about your brother; all you wanted was him out of the picture, and you'd have all the money in the company, and Kenai would get nothing."

"My brother deserved nothing; that's why our father left the company to me. So yes, the company is mine. If anything happened to me, it would go to my wife and daughter."

"Before you hang up, my wife asked me to see if you will allow Mia to spend the summer with her cousin. That's Julia, in case you forgot her name? I know it's probably out of the question based on the situation, but it would mean a lot to Cadence. I can tell her you've already made other plans for the summer."

"I am done talking with you. I must go; my break is up. Talk to you later." Jocelyn stuffed her phone in her uniform pocket.

After finishing up the last flight for the evening, she'd left for home. She had been dreading the other news she needed to break to her mother. Once she arrived home, she could hear her mother and daughter in the kitchen getting dinner ready as her mother did every day. She gave a quick hello to them and dashed off upstairs to take a shower.

After showering, they all had dinner, then Jocelyn put Mia to bed, but her daughter was fussy and didn't want to go to sleep. After reading a story to her, she'd drifted off to a night of deep sleep. Jocelyn and her mother met up in the living room and had coffee.

"Mother, these last few weeks have been tough for me. Working long hours and not getting to spend any time with my daughter is too much. I have made a change that I know you will not like."

"What sort of change, Jocelyn? I know you're not thinking about marrying that guy after one date."

Jocelyn laughed. "No, not that drastic, mother."

"Mother, please don't get upset by what I am going to tell you because I think it's best for Mia and me."

"First, I appreciate all you do for us. You've done more than any daughter could ask. However, I've decided that when Mia is out of school for the summer, we will move to Hawaii. They have offered me a promotion with Delta Airlines, and I will work there as a manager, and

I'll have time to get Mia enrolled in school before it starts for the new year."

"I knew something was going on with you, but I never guessed this. I thought you were happy here. How will you afford to live there on your salary?"

"Mother, I would be a manager, and there would be an enormous increase in my salary. I'm getting help from Tyler, and the cost of living there is less than Fairbanks."

"Did you make a deal with that devil of a brother-in-law, and have you discussed this with Mia? Have you thought about how it will affect her by not being around her grandmother?"

"No, to everything you asked. It's time to get out on my own and take care of Mia. I need to start some sort of permanent life, as you say."

"Are you going there with that Alphonso guy?"

"No."

"I think you're making a mistake. Is there another man involved that you haven't told me about?"

"There's nobody else involved; it is just my daughter and me."

"You are an adult, so I can't stop you. But I wish you'd think about it some more before you decide. Sit down and have a talk with Mia before you make a firm decision."

"I'm going to do that this weekend before going on vacation. I'm going to bed. I have another twelve-hour day tomorrow. Goodnight, Mother."

"Goodnight. I love you, Jocelyn."

"Love you back, Mother."

Jocelyn couldn't let her mother know that she'd only make all this possible for her and Mia by doing something illegal.

Chapter Twelve

FAMILY AND MONEY

Every time he got involved with Jocelyn, bad things happened. But business was business, and she's just the dumb honey he needed to get the job done. With her future riding on this deal, he'd get her to do anything.

Tyler and his wife were waiting for their daughter Julia in the dining room of their Pensacola home. They did this as often as possible. Tyler was in turmoil because everything he and his father had worked for all their lives was in jeopardy. He didn't know how to break the awful news to his wife. His father wouldn't be proud of him, and he knew his grandparents wouldn't be either.

His wife, Cadence, was an excellent cook, a noble companion, wife, and wonderful mother. She's the best thing that had ever happened in his life, and he didn't deserve her. Not only was he in financial trouble, but he's trying to avenge the past for his grandparents.

Because of this real estate business, he's away from his family for long periods. The parenting of his daughter was up to his wife. Whenever he's home, he didn't change the ground rules she had in place for discipline. His brother, Kenai, had tried to date his wife before he'd married Jocelyn, but Cadence was too smart to get mixed up with Kenai.

He'd given his family everything they needed. But he'd made some dirty deals in the past, and they'd cost the company financially. If he didn't pull this deal off, he would lose the company, their home, and go bankrupt. The company was in trouble when his dad died, but he'd tried to keep things afloat.

He'd changed the name of the company from RTK, LLC to Hailer, LLC. The initials RTK represented R for Robert, his father, T for Tyler, and K for Kenai. Kenai didn't work for the company while his father lived and did even less after his death. Tyler, the current CEO, didn't want his brother's name to be part of the brand. The project he's currently working on for Hailer, LLC was not in Pensacola. He'd hoped that his father's past political connections in Alaska would help him make a deal that could save the company.

He'd made a financial deal with a friend to gain some Alaska properties, but it proved unsuccessful. That same friend was threatening to sue, but it would get thrown out of court because it was his idea. Tyler was trying the same deal on his own, but with a fresh approach and other people. The low-lives he'd hired would do anything for money. Tyler had worked alongside his father, learning everything about the business, while Kenai did nothing but reaped full benefits. After his father died, his brother wanted to continue taking dividends from the company and not have to work for it, but Tyler wouldn't allow it.

His brother's wife, Jocelyn, and his family had a good relationship while their parents lived, but it had soured since his brother's death. Tyler wouldn't let her know, but he'd understood why Jocelyn cheated on his brother. Kenai was not good to her. He'd only wanted to be married for the namesake and to reap the benefits of that, too.

The only thing his brother was passionate about was hunting moose. He and his wife lived near Jocelyn's mother. And there were lots of woods. It was easy for him to pursue as often as he wanted to. Kenai's relationship fell apart before their daughter was born, and by the time she'd arrived, it was irreparable. But he was crazy about his daughter.

She'd brought out something in him that Tyler had never seen.

Before his brother died, Jocelyn called several times, needing money. He'd always did what he could to help. Early on a Saturday morning, six years ago, his brother was hunting with friends when his gun backfired, killing him.

There was a trial, and the police accused Jocelyn of his murder. She had an excellent lawyer that got her off. Tyler didn't know how she paid her attorney fees and, he'd assumed that her mother paid them. The autopsy results showed that Kenai had been drinking, and something that he'd called limp-wristing had caused the accident. Wristing occurs if a shooter doesn't hold a firearm firmly enough. It causes the weapon to not function fully, and it backfires on the shooter.

A couple of years after Kenai's death, Tyler received a call from Jocelyn asking for money. She'd wanted to get her and Mia out of Alaska and move to Hawaii. Tyler was sad for his niece Mia every time he'd thought about how vindictive her mother was. Jocelyn wanted to move out of the house with her mother. It was great timing for Tyler because he'd needed her help on a particular project. He saw an opportunity to use the situation to his advantage. She's desperate to get what she'd wanted and would do anything for money. She's putty in his hands and agreed to carry out her part in a deal regarding a real-estate transfer.

His daughter ran to the table and startled him.

"Honey, it is so good to be home, so I can have dinner with my favorite two people. Soon we'll be able to do this more often."

"Is that a promise? We're glad you're here, as well. I cooked your favorites tonight because I don't know when we will do this again. Your being at home this week has been good for all three of us." Cadence smiled. Tyler knew if she's happy, everything would be okay.

"I have seen you smiling more this week than in the past six months." Tyler hugged his wife and daughter to him.

"Why don't the three of us go to the beach tomorrow. We haven't done that in a long time. Does that sound like a good idea, baby?" Tyler suggested.

"Yes, daddy. I love going to the beach, and I can wear the new swimsuit that Mommy bought for me."

"What color is it."

"Mommy, what color is it?" Julia asked.

"It's pink and white, honey."

"Baby, that sounds so pretty. We'll get out early in the morning before it gets crowded and hot on the beach."

"Tyler, you seem to be worried about something. Is everything okay at the office, honey?"

"Nothing different from any other week. We just had a bump in the road with the new project I told you about. People don't always do what they are supposed to, and they take matters into their own hands and run it the way they want. I'll need to make a few phone calls after dinner."

"I've been thinking about Jocelyn and Mia. We haven't seen them in a long time. Maybe we can get her to bring Mia to spend the summer with us," Cadence inquired.

"What a coincidence. I talked to Jocelyn earlier today and mentioned to her about spending some time with our daughter. She said her job had her working long hours, so it would not be possible this summer. And, since I'm such a wonderful husband, and since we have finished eating, I'll help you with the dishes."

"No, you make your calls. I can manage, and your daughter enjoys washing dishes, unlike her father. When we finish, I'll bathe her and put her to bed; then we can have some alone time?"

"Okay, I won't be long. I'll use the phone in my office."

After talking to Jocelyn, he figured he had to call officer Connor to get an update.

Officer Connor Wynn in the Anchorage Police Department answered his cell on the third ring.

"Hello, my friend. I need you to tell me that things are under control, and you've a handle on our arrangement."

"Everything is under control and in place," Connor said.

"Call me if anything changes. Goodbye."

"Will do." They hang up without saying their names or mentioning specific details.

Officer Connor was the one person he'd count on. He did what you instructed him to do and promptly.

Tyler could get back to his wife and maybe get to read a bedtime story to his daughter. He'd missed the time to bond with her as a father and daughter should.

Chapter Thirteen

POLICE CORRUPTION

Anchorage had the largest police department in Alaska. It also has the highest crime rate and corruption of any city in the state. Officer Connor was one of their best and was up for promotion to Sergeant. He'd spent three hours questioning a suspect for the Hotel International-A threat case. Connor had transported all the evidence that was gathered and processed to the crime scene at the precinct. His partner Officer Layla asked him about his tactics before he'd took the suspect into custody. They worked together in the crime prevention unit and lacked evidence for this incident. Therefore, Connor okayed releasing the suspect with his Sergeant.

Now in the break room, getting coffee with his partner, they swapped some unpleasant words.

"Next time you have a problem with the way I question a suspect, speak to me about it. If you go behind my back again, I will request a new partner, Officer Layla."

"It's clear we didn't attend the same police academy because the one I graduated from says a witness or suspect should never be questioned without a second officer present. Whether it's in a witness room at the department or off-site. Having two officers present protects the witness and the officers. The next time you do it that way, I will report you up the chain of command. You will not disrespect me because I'm a woman.

I know the standards of conduct as well as anyone here, and that includes you. You have a nice day."

"Hold on, Layla. You have this all wrong. Either that or you misunderstood my intentions. I wanted you outside the room at the hotel to ensure we would not be disturbed. I felt we'd get more information from the suspect if we questioned him in a familiar environment instead of at the police department. We had to secure the witness and the scene right away. It was nothing else."

"While you were doing things your way, maybe you didn't notice that the hotel owner had her legal representatives there. It didn't go unnoticed, and they felt your actions were strange, too. You acted in an unprofessional manner. They thought you should've taken the suspect to the police department and not have him locked away alone in a back room of the hotel to question him. The implications of misconduct are massive. For all we know, you could've threatened the suspect, paid him off, or people could even conclude that you and the suspect are in this crime together," Layla said.

"Have you any idea how ridiculous that sounds?"

"It sounds like common sense to me, and I'd stand by my concerns. I had to explain to the representatives what you were doing. Don't let it happen again on my watch. Good day."

Connor didn't need this while he's in line for a promotion. He'd keep his eye on Layla from now on and be more careful. She'd cost him his job.

His burner phone rang, so he knew it was Tyler. He'd went outside the building to talk to him.

"Hello Tyler, how are things going."

"I called to ask you the same thing. It's reported that you arrested someone today."

"I question him to ensure no one else found out what he's doing.

He did things exactly as instructed, and he knew what the consequences were. He was careful not to leave any fingerprints. The hotel is under thirty-day police protection, though. An order our Chief of Police had signed by the judge. We'll have to be careful in the future. Is it worth it to continue?" Connor asked.

"Are you scared? You're in too deep to back out now. You see it through. In the end, there's a big payoff for you." Tyler reminded him.

"What's going to happen when our friend finds out we're doing things behind her back?" Connor asked.

"Let me handle that, and I'll do whatever I need to when the time comes."

"There were some investigators here today. They're representing the hotel. We have to work with them, based on orders from the Chief of Police."

"That could complicate things. Now I see why you want to be cautious about how we move forward," Tyler said.

"Tyler, you know I can lose my job and everything I've worked for the past few years?"

"You should've thought about that before you turned to the dark side, and went rogue, my friend. But don't worry, that's not going to happen."

"I have to get back to work. I will keep you abreast of any updates when they happen."

"I am counting on you. Make sure we only talk on the burner phones." Tyler reminded him.

Chapter Fourteen

UNEXPECTED DEVELOPMENT

It's finally Friday morning, and Alphonso was happy because he's going on vacation with Jocelyn on Monday. But on a sad note, Amelia had another threat to her life. She's dependent on Soco & Soco and the police to bring closure to the dangers.

Based on the phone call he had from Liam the night before, not only did they have to be concerned about civilians, but there may be police corruption with the case. Alphonso needed a better understanding of the situation in his team meeting that morning. He'd felt like a hypocrite going on vacation with a stranger when Amelia needed his help. She's still his friend.

Arriving at the office at his usual time, he'd parked his car, walked into the law firm in a trance-like state, and passed by Joan's desk without saying good morning.

"Good morning, Alphonso. Aren't you going to speak to me today?" Joan asked.

Startled and nervous, he said. "Good morning, Joan. I'm sorry. It's one of those mornings, and I've a lot on my mind."

"You've been walking past this desk for many years and saying good morning before going to your office. I will forgive you this one time. Are you okay?"

"With the case involving Amelia, trying to plan a vacation, meetings today, and outstanding actions I need to complete by day's end, it's taken a toll on me. I didn't mean to ignore you."

"You need this vacation. Hopefully, when you come back, we can have a normal greeting."

"That's a promise."

It's ten-thirty. He's finishing a summary from a different case to pass onto Joan for legal formatting to submit to Jason. James and Noah come in for a briefing before meeting with the Soco brothers.

"Come on in, and let's talk at the conference table."

"I read the briefing you sent last night. Are there any additional updates or changes that I should know?"

"After speaking with Liam, we've been speculating," James stated.

"What about?" Asked Alphonso.

"We believe officer Connor may be in on this threat, but we've not figured out how yet. The suspect was only at the station for three hours and then released."

"If this is true, we have to warn Amelia. Let's see if we can get in to see Jason and Jermaine now. This can't wait."

Alphonso called Jason. "Hello Alphonso, are you calling to cancel the meeting?"

"There's been a development, and we need to speak with you now."

"Okay, meet me in the conference room, and I'll get Jermaine."

When they were all present, they sat around the table.

Alphonso opened the meeting and gave the brothers an explanation of their concerns and how the new speculation could affect Amelia. Jason and Jermaine agreed and decided it was urgent enough to warn her. Alphonso called her.

The phone rang three times before she answered.

"Hello, Alphonso; how are you?"

"Amelia, Are you alone?"

"Yes, I just got out of a meeting with my hotel security."

"Amelia, we are assembled at the firm because we have something urgent to discuss with you and your security. Can you get them in your office for this conference call and alert them that they will be on speaker?"

Within five minutes, they were all ready for the call. "Alphonso, we are here. What's wrong?"

"Hi Amelia. Jason, Jermaine, and James are here with me. We believe that officer Connor Wynn and your employee Evan are in on this threat together. Until we can identify the evidence and get this case solved, we recommend putting Evan on leave. He's desperate for some reason and might do anything to cover his tracks. Additionally, we suggest your security stay near, twenty-four hours a day," Alphonso explained their concerns.

With a tremble in her voice, Amelia said, "This is scaring me even more than I already was. Evan has a wife and children and will go quietly to spend more time with them. There's no problem putting him on extended leave with pay. By doing it that way, I protect the hotel liability."

"We're going to provide additional service with the brother's consent. Noah, one of our investigators, will get a room at your hotel for however long is necessary. He'll be your additional eyes and ears to what's going on at the hotel. Noah will monitor police officer Connor's activity. We advise he poses as a staff member and that you put him in a staff uniform either in housekeeping or as a concierge. Be aware that he's licensed to carry, but it will not be visible. Maybe that will give you some additional peace of mind. He'll introduce himself to you upon arrival."

"That would be great. Thank you all again for the monumental work you have completed already. I'm glad I chose this firm."

"We'll continue our investigation and look into the matters we've discussed today. Whatever else comes up, we'll contact you immediately. We ask that your security notify us right away if there's any suspicious activity. We'll contact Connor's Chief to do some digging, but at present, we don't know how deep this corruption has expanded. For that reason, we'll be treading with caution. I think we've covered all the bases. We know it can't be easy but try to go about as normally as you can. Goodbye, Amelia."

"I know that what I just said to Amelia about sending an investigator to check into the hotel was a surprise, and I'd hope I didn't overstep my bounds. Noah would be the ideal person for this task because nobody at the hotel or the precinct where police officer Connor works has seen him. Noah, I'd hope this doesn't interfere with any plans you may have."

"No, it's okay. I quite fancy myself as a concierge; if the pay's better there, I might stay on." They all laughed.

"I see Alphonso's sense of humor has rubbed off on his team," Jason said.

"Did you say vacation? If someone offered me a free one, it would be wonderful," Alphonso said with a wink.

"Putting the joking aside, Alphonso, what you've suggested is a great idea. Noah, you'll probably be at Amelia's hotel for a few days. I'll have Joan make the arrangements and have everything you need to charge the firm's credit card. If you spend anything out of pocket, please fill out a voucher, and we'll take care of it. I would like for you to leave first thing in the morning."

"We want you to be eyes and ears not only for the hotel but for the firm as well. You should present yourself like a normal employee, which will give you access to all areas of the hotel without arousing suspicion. You can ask which room Amelia is in and meet with her security personal upon arrival. Alphonso, you'll be indisposed for the next few days, but we'll keep you updated if there are any developments. Is there anything else since we had a planned briefing?"

"From our research of the threats, we've found that there may be three companies. The only difference is that these companies have had projects like this case, but without the threats. One each in Alaska, New York, and Pensacola. To reemphasize, we need to determine what's Connor's role,." Alphonso explained. "My sideshow interview in Pensacola will determine if Amelia's brother is involved in the threats. Once those issues are verified, we'll be close to solving the case. What's puzzling me is that the targeted area is thriving for tourism. Why would anyone want to demolish a hotel to replace it with apartments or condos? There must be some underlining reason for these actions."

"My brother and I agree with you and your team assessment Alphonso. You've done an outstanding job in less than a week, and each of you is the reason we continue to be a great law firm," Jason said.

"That sounds like a pay raise speech to me." Alphonso quipped back at him.

"Man, I keep telling you, comedy is not you're calling."

"Let's get back to work. Alphonso, you have a glorious trip to Pensacola, and keep us posted if you find any additional evidence. We want to see a tan in a few days, and Noah, watch your back," Jason concluded.

Alphonso was sitting at his desk and was surprised that the brothers went along with his suggestion. He'd generally consult them before making a significant decision that called for spending money. He's glad they had that confidence in him. His only task before going home was a summary of all that had taken place that week with the case and forward it to the brothers and Liam. Alphonso felt better about the case and what he and his team had uncovered.

Chapter Fifteen

IN HIS BACKYARD

Alphonso wasn't used to sleeping in late on a Saturday morning after staying up so late on Friday night. He'd quickly get used to it. Maybe that could be something for him and his future wife to enjoy. What a draining week it had been. He's ready for his vacation with Jocelyn but concerned for Amelia's safety. He'd sat on the side of the bed for five minutes before dragging himself up. He had a shower and went to the kitchen to fix breakfast.

Afterward, he'd did that same dreadful thing as most people on Saturday. He washed his clothes and cleaned up his home. He's a neat freak, and nothing in his condo was out of place. But that was because he lived alone. He'd pack his clothes for Monday. And then he'd relax on Sunday and have the last check on Monday morning to ensure he didn't forget to pack something.

Alphonso wondered if Amelia was awake at this hour. If you managed a hotel, your day most likely started early, so he called her. Amelia was up and having a cup of coffee, as well. Alphonso wondered if she'd be hesitant about answering the phone because of the threats.

"Hello, this is Amelia?"

"Amelia, this is Alphonso, and it sounds like you are awake."

"Yes, I am. What can I do for you on this beautiful Saturday morning?"

"I woke up thinking about what you've been through and just wanted to give you some encouragement."

"I hope you're right because right now, I see nothing changing. I'm confident that your firm is doing everything possible to solve this, and knowing that you are on the case comforts me, too."

"I promise you; it'll be over soon."

"You are optimistic, and that is good."

"I haven't seen your investigator Noah yet, but knowing he's coming makes me feel safe. He's leaving this morning, so he should be here sometime early afternoon."

"I'd like to talk to you about another subject that has been on my mind since I saw you at the firm. After high school, I felt that we never had proper closure to our relationship. You were busy working at your family's hotel. And I was too young and impatient to give you the time you needed to find balance in your life. I believe because of that, we were torn apart. Can you explain it to me? I know it's been a long time. If you don't want to talk about it, I am okay with that."

"Alphonso, I have thought about you a lot over the years and wondered where you were and what you were doing. I know we didn't have closure, and I apologize. Working at the hotel gave me a tremendous responsibility at a young age. I missed out on a lot during my teenage years and through college. Because of my parents' expectations, I couldn't develop a relationship with anyone. All I have known is work, even though my parents are no longer here. I don't even know if I can develop a lasting relationship. I hope that answers your question."

"Yes, it does. My life in the workforce has kept me busy, as well. I have not focused on a relationship, either. I've tried to be the best investigator that I can be."

"From what I am hearing, you are the best in the area, and some other states, as well."

"So, you've been checking up on me, then?" They both laughed.

"You can call it that. I did research your firm, and so far, I'm not disappointed."

"I'm glad that you're pleased with our work. Next week I'll be out of the office, but my team are the best. If anything comes up, they'll contact me. So have a wonderful Saturday, and I'll talk to you soon."

"Good talking to you, as well. Have a wonderful weekend, and call anytime. Goodbye, Alphonso."

"You do the same. Goodbye."

Alphonso felt good after his conversation with Amelia. He had answers about their past relationship. She might even be interested in a relationship after this case was over. Not necessarily a relationship with him, but with someone.

He did not need to call Jocelyn because he'd already coordinated a pickup time on Monday for 6:30 a.m. for their vacation. The flight was due to leave at 8:30 a.m.

Alphonso hit the fitness center in his community for a couple of hours. Work had kept him so busy that week, he hadn't been at all. Usually, Alphonso would go at least twice a week. He'd need to get back on his game for exercising upon return because he had gained five pounds the last time he went on the scales. Not good. During his workout, he'd noticed there were several ladies he'd never seen before. One of them kept looking at him, so he waved. If he wasn't getting ready for a vacation with another woman, he'd check them out. After his explosive workout, he washed his favorite car.

His community activity committee planned a karaoke night that evening at the clubhouse. He'd attend and expose his singing talents. In a newsletter, the community management had alerted residents that too many condos were vacant and for sale. He'd have a chat with the community manager at tonight's gathering to determine the cause.

Alphonso strolled in the event at 8:30 p.m. and was surprised so many people were there. He and several residents grouped together and knocked out some karaoke favorites. It turned out to be a blast. He'd spotted the manager.

"Hello, Cindy. I see a lot of residents are leaving the community. Can you give me some insight?"

"Hello, Alphonso. You rocked tonight, man."

"I've a few hidden talents."

"I haven't seen you the last few months. I thought some young thing had swopped you up and convinced you to turn in your single card."

"No, not quite, but I am looking."

"To answer your question. Some real estate developers from out of state buy up all the condos in anticipation of live work and play areas. Whoever it is, they're paying the residents top dollar. I'm not sure how they are making any money, but that is the scoop."

"That's interesting. Would you know who it might be?" Alphonso asked.

"Whoever they are, they're tight-lipped in their planning."

"I had a great time tonight, and everything was nice, as always." "Thank you. I have an early morning flight. See you later."

That was excellent information. Alphonso wonders if these are the same developers trying to force Amelia out. Still, Cindy didn't say people were being forced out. The culprit might be right here in his backyard.

After returning to his condo, he'd went to bed right away and had a horrifying dream about the beach. He'd shrugged it off. On Sunday morning, he got up early, had a cup of coffee, put on his swimming trunks, and went for a swim in the community pool. This would be the next best thing to being at the beach. He'd thought that going as soon as it opened, no one would be there, but boy was he wrong. Some other residents had the same idea. He'd felt like a lone wolf in the forest since he's the only male there, and he's not even on the hunt.

After several laps, he'd returned home. He took a ride to the mall and picked up some new swimming trunks for his trip tomorrow, and he'd ate lunch at the food court in the mall. Then he went back home to finish his packing. He'd watched a couple of movies, marked his calendar for the search of his soulmate, and was in bed by 9 p.m.

Chapter Sixteen

LONG AWAITED VACATION

Alphonso's vacation day finally arrived. It was a journey with Jocelyn involving eating lots of seafood, staying up late every night, enjoying the beach, and coming up with whatever else they came up with. He'd dashed out of bed, sprinted through the shower, and slipped on his traveling clothes. After a coffee and toast for breakfast, he's ready to take on the day. Before leaving, he'd marked another day on his calendar. He ensured all the lights were out in the condo except the dining room.

At six twenty-five, he'd arrived at Jocelyn's. He pulled into the driveway, and the garage door opened. A beautiful female, about five feet tall, stepped out with a cute carry-on bag.

"Hello, I'm Alphonso. You must be Joycelyn's mother."

"Yes, I'm Ava. It's about time we met. Take care of my girl; she's my only child."

"Yes, ma'am, I will. It's a pleasure to meet you."

Jocelyn came out with her suitcase. Man, does she look hot in her pink shorts with a pink and white top, and she's leaving with him.

"Hi, Alphonso. I see you have met my mom. What terrible stories has she told you?"

"Hello, Jocelyn. She just wants me to take care of her only daughter."

"Mom, I will call you when we get there. I love you."

"Love you, too, honey."

Alphonso stacked her baggage in the trunk while Jocelyn finished her goodbyes. She appeared to have a good relationship with her mother. Alphonso liked that. It's a good sign.

"Have fun. Do nothing I wouldn't do."

"What did she mean by that comment?" Alphonso asked.

"Don't let you take advantage of me. It is just a figure of speech. Nothing to worry about."

"In the eyes of our mothers, we never grow up."

"You're right. My mom is a worrier. But she'll do anything for me and asks no questions. I love her very much."

"Make sure you keep that relationship."

"Spending time with my mom helps me keep a perspective."

"How has your morning been so far, Jocelyn?"

"You make me laugh, it's barely half-past six, and it's hardly started. I was awake early this morning because the excitement of our trip kept me up late. Long hours at work for the last two months have been exhausting. This trip is going to be a welcome break to relax and have some fun. What about you?"

"Last week was so draining that when I woke this morning, it felt like a supercharge. I knew this break would help. Thank you for coming with me, Jocelyn."

"We both needed a boost, and spending it together makes it special."

"A friend of mine called Sam used to work in long-term airport parking. He'd moved to Delta Junction to take care of his wife after she suffered a stroke. I'd always felt my car was safe, no matter how long I was away when he was there. Let's find a parking spot close to check-in. What are your friends going to think about checking us in together?"

"They won't ignite until we're out of sight. But they'll have a million questions when we return. When we walk up, make sure you have a big smile on your face to show them how handsome you are. I want to make them jealous."

After checking in at the departure counter, Alphonso and Jocelyn went to the security checkpoint.

"Glad we survived the check-in with my airline friends," Jocelyn said with a smile.

"It wasn't so bad. I got to meet one of your friends who was checking me out from head to toe."

"We'll be the topic in the break room for a few days."

"The security check-in is what I hate most about flying. For all the things you must remove, you might as well walk through naked. But once you walk through, supposedly, within a few seconds, they can find anything suspicious. If that's true, why do people get through security with things they tell you not to bring?" Alphonso asked.

"I've no answer, but glad we have the security. Airport security personnel save lives every day."

"Since you speak from that perspective, I won't complain."

"I like this airport is not huge compared to Hartsfield Jackson in Atlanta, and some other airports. You can easily get lost if you don't know where you are going in them."

"Maybe someday I will fly to Atlanta with you. That may push my luck," Jocelyn said.

"No, that's okay, and we never know what will happen in the future. We have a twelve-hour flight which includes stops and layovers in Seattle, Washington, and Atlanta, before reaching our destination in Pensacola, Florida, at 8:30 p.m. I'm glad we have first-class tickets; it makes it faster to board. You can relax, have a cocktail, and get acquainted with your flight attendant before all the other passenger's board."

"You're a kind man, Alphonso. You make flying sound so exciting, but I've flown little lately."

"When you trained to become an airline attendant, did going

through security and some of the other protocols concerning passengers come into play?"

"No, it didn't. Our training was all about customer service, greeting, and procedures for handling troublesome passengers if we encounter them, and safety. No one has disrespected me in all the years I've worked for Delta."

"You must enjoy your job."

"I do, but I can picture myself in a management role, which would increase my annual income. I'm looking at some opportunities that may allow me to fulfill my goal, but it will call for a transfer."

"That is great, Jocelyn."

Alphonso is in seat 3B, an aisle seat, and Jocelyn in 3A with a window view. Once seated and buckled in their seatbelts, the flight attendant greeted them with a glass of white wine. Shortly afterward, all passengers were boarded, and the plane was ready for takeoff.

"You said you haven't flown in a while. Are you nervous about flying?" Alphonso asked.

"I don't think so, but we'll know in a few minutes."

"Would you like me to hold your hand?"

"That would be nice. I took a Dramamine pill, so I should be okay. You sitting next to me makes me feel better."

"Okay, we are ready to go." With a smile on his face, Alphonso thought they were off to a wonderful start.

"Are you okay, Jocelyn?"

"Yes, everything is okay. I'm looking forward to having a mind-free week of vacation away from work."

"This is the first visit to Pensacola for both of us. We can explore it together."

"Ah, I forgot to tell you. I came to Pensacola about five years ago with a friend. We didn't get to the beach because it rained the entire time. I was only there for a weekend."

"Oh, I thought you'd have mentioned that. Anyway, I can't wait to get to the beach." With a half-grin on his face, he'd wondered what else she'd forgotten to tell him. Alphonso had a similar reaction from Jason when he told him Jocelyn was going with him to Pensacola. It wasn't like Jason. Ordinarily, he's optimistic about everything and had often said that Alphonso needed a girlfriend. What was he missing?

"Since I was up so early this morning, would it bother you if I had a quick nap, we have a long flight?"

"No, I'll have one, too. And, by the time we wake up, the flight attendant will have a snack for us. I brought a book to help pass the time."

Alphonso retrieved a folder out of his laptop bag concerning the Amelia case while she slept. He'd glanced over his notes, trying to figure out what motivated a developer to want the land where the hotel sat. Why disrupt a booming sector of the city? Then he'd found out over the weekend that his community might be caught in this web.

These companies could be in trouble financially, or somebody could blackmail the other. One of them had political connections at the state and local levels. He'd drifted into a deep sleep after this exhaustive thinking.

Within forty-five minutes, they both awoke and went to the restroom. They both had a snack.

"How is your food, Jocelyn?"

"To my surprise, the food is tasty. Over the years, they've improved the taste and added more choices. Which is good when you're on a long trip. This flight is a learning experience for me. I know nothing about the operations and what goes into preparing a flight for passengers. I can appreciate it and better understand passengers and flight attendant's complaints and concerns. I'll have a fresh perspective when back at work. How about your job? Do you like it?"

"I give a hundred per cent every day. Sometimes it is exhausting, but I enjoy solving cases, no matter what it involves."

"Going by our conversations, you know more about Soco firm than the average Alaskan."

"I don't think so. I just like to take an interest."

Alphonso noticed she spoke with an attitude and the conversation lapsed into an awkward pause.

The pilot announced they would arrive in Seattle in forty-five minutes. They had the same seats for each leg of their trip.

"It didn't feel like a long flight from Alaska. It could be because we took a nap. I feel better about it. What about you, Jocelyn? Are you okay?"

"I feel the same way. The quicker we get to our destination, the better. Then we can have some fun."

"Seattle has a lot of rain at this time of year and normally gets one hundred and fifty-two days of it a year. The driest months are July through August. I guess we got lucky traveling in May." Alphonso knew he caused offense earlier and tried to get them back on track with light conversation.

"Why does it have to rain so much?"

"I think it's because Seattle is in the direct path of moisture from the Pacific Ocean."

"Yes, I get that. Given what you've told me, it's not on my list of favorite places to visit."

After a four-hour layover in Seattle, the flight to Atlanta, and another layover, they were on the last leg of their trip to Pensacola. Exhausted from all-day traveling, they were ready for some rest.

"The Atlanta airport was stunning and huge, as you said, and I'm glad I had time to see some of it."

"It is one-fourth of a mile to each concourse. That's why so many people take the train to get to their respective gates."

"Finally, here we are at our destination." Alphonso smiled.

"Thank goodness, I'm so drained."

"You will have the rest of the night after we get some dinner and as much time as you want tomorrow to relax."

"To heck with relaxing, I'm checking out the beach first thing in the morning," Jocelyn said with excitement.

"I'd plan on getting there as soon as possible tomorrow."

There's no wait time for picking up their rental car, and soon they were on their way to the hotel.

"What a beautiful drive at night from the airport, especially driving on the Bayfront parkway across the Pensacola bay bridge," Jocelyn said.

"You're right; it's exquisite. There's a restaurant I'm going to take you to called Peg Legs. It's near our hotel. Shorts and a top will be fine, the dress code is casual, and that's what I'm going to wear. We can go there for dinner once we've checked into our rooms if that is okay with you. I'm starving. When I was doing my research for restaurants in the area, Peg Legs was number one on the lists. They've live music if you fancy dancing your dinner off, later."

"I only have the energy to eat tonight. The restaurant sounds interesting, especially the name. I hope they have seafood?"

"Yes, they are famous for their oysters on the half-shell. There's something for anyone who visits, including children. How long will you need to get ready before going for dinner?"

"About twenty minutes. I'll freshen up after the long trip and text you when I'm ready."

"Okay. Take as much time as you need. The restaurant is open late."

They checked in at the front desk, got to their suites, and freshened up. Jocelyn made a quick call to let her mother know they'd arrived safely. Within minutes, they were in the car on their way to dinner.

"How's your room?"

"It's large enough for two or three people, but nice. The beach is within walking distance. You made a brilliant choice, Alphonso."

"Thank you. Glad the room is okay. Mine is roomy and nice as well. My appointment tomorrow is at eleven a.m. Would you like to have breakfast together in the hotel? I'll be out for two hours for my appointment."

"Yes, that's perfect. Then afterward, I'll transform into a beach goer."

"We can have lunch at the beach if you like, some restaurants are within walking distance. Then we'll make plans after that."

"Sounds great."

Jocelyn livened up once they arrived at the restaurant.

The one thing they seemed to have in common was wine. Once seated, that's what both ordered as a beverage. "Wow, this place rocks. There's still a long line waiting outside. The music sounds great coming from downstairs," Jocelyn said, with a smile from cheek to cheek. Alphonso relaxed and sang along with the music.

"The music has a good beat. I wonder who the artists are. It sounds like a man and woman singing. You don't sound too bad yourself."

"Thank you. The restaurant owner has another venue: A Marina where you can hire a boat and sail to it."

"That sounds exciting arriving in a boat to get your dinner."

"We can do it later in the week if we like the food tonight."

They had a dozen oysters as an appetizer, and a mixed grill for entrees, with a second glass of white wine.

"I like the layout of the restaurant. They've a special area for children to play. It's a very relaxed atmosphere, and the casual dress makes you feel comfortable, too. The food is perfect, and the company."

"Glad to hear that everything is okay, including me. And the rest of the trip will soar after we rest. Are you ready to go back to the hotel, maybe a quick brandy for a nightcap in the bar before we call it a night?"

"Yes, I am ready, and the brandy would be just the right nightcap." Alphonso paid the bill, and they were on their way. Back at the hotel, they sat in the bar for an hour and then said their goodnights.

As Alphonso was entering his room, when he got a call on his cell phone. It wasn't a number he'd recognized.

"Hello."

"Hi, Alphonso, this is William. How are you?"

"I am fine, thanks, and you. I'm just getting in from dinner. How can I help you?"

"I'm afraid something's come up, and I need to change our appointment from eleven to ten a.m. Hopefully, it doesn't affect any plans you have tomorrow?"

"No, that would be great. I'm on vacation, so it's better for me, too. I'll see you, then. Goodbye."

He wondered why William wanted to change their appointment. Regardless, it was good news and meant he'd spend more time with Jocelyn in the morning. He called to let her know the time change. "Hi again, Jocelyn. Thank you for a beautiful evening."

"No, I should thank you. Is anything wrong?"

"No, just a change of plans. My meeting changed to ten in the morning, so we could have an early breakfast, or you can sleep in late.'

"I think I will take you up on the sleep in late."

"That is fine. Charge anything you need to the room. If you get up early, I was told the hotel has great massage treatments here. I want you to relax and enjoy everything available."

"I'll see how I feel in the morning."

"I'll be back by one, and if anything changes, I'll call you. Sleep well, Jocelyn."

"Okay, you, too."

Chapter Seventeen

THE INTERVIEWS

Alphonso ordered room service, giving him more time to prepare for his meeting with William. He wondered what kind of business he was involved with. He arrived at a small office with a sign on the door advertising Pensacola's Best Tours, in good time.

Alphonso went in and introduced himself to the receptionist.

"Can I speak to William, please?" Before he could get his name out, William strode over to greet him.

"Hello. I'm William Haley. Did you have a problem finding us?"

"No, the directions were straightforward enough."

"Glad you didn't have any problems. You must be Alphonso Lott?"

"Yes, I am."

"Follow me to my office. Have a seat."

"I know you have a busy schedule, so thank you for seeing me this morning. I didn't realize you ran a tourist business. It must keep you busy this time of year."

"Oh, it does. I started this business a few years ago and have four employees. We specialize in tours that take you to places you would never know about otherwise. The tourist business here is good year-round, and it's an honest living for someone like me who doesn't enjoy working too hard."

"That's great. As you know, I'm here to discuss the hotel and have a few questions, but I promise not to keep you long. When we spoke on the phone the other day, I explained that your sister had been getting death threats. They've escalated this week, and we need to understand it. Why did you want Amelia to sell the hotel when it's doing so well?"

"Excuse me? I'm picking up from your tone that you're trying to lay a guilt trip on me. My sister probably didn't inform you of her concerns about the hotel's survival after my parents died. She never told me she didn't want to sell, and it was always a case of just tossing ideas around to see what was going to be best for both of us," William said.

"I've looked over the financials, and the net income has never been stronger; it seems to be an unwise time to sell. Over the past five years, major upgrades brought it up to today's standards. Someone is trying to force Amelia to sell. Were you aware of that?"

"No, I wasn't. We don't talk often. And clearly, if we were going to sell, and that was only ever an idea, we would do it when the hotel was turning a good profit to get the best price."

"And yet, just months after you couldn't convince her to sell, the threats began. Let's not beat about the bush. I'm going to put a very blunt question to you. Can you honestly say that you aren't working with anyone to force her out? And before you jump all over me, maybe you aren't aware of their extreme methods. Do you have any enemies in Alaska or Pensacola that influenced the real estate business? What about your parents? Did they have any enemies, someone that would do anything to get what they want, even to the point of killing your sister if necessary?"

William was furious. Alphonso had poked him with a stick to gauge his reaction. He saw William trying to control his facial expressions and failing.

"I love my sister very much. She is the only family I have. How dare you accuse me of partnering to have her killed? You think someone will take her life because she won't commit to selling the hotel? I think you've been reading too many storybooks, my friend. Now, I'm busy and have work to do, so if there's nothing else."

"For her safety, Amelia has moved into the hotel under the protection of hotel security and the police. I'm not trying to upset you, but to let you know how real this situation is, and if there's something you know that could help to save Amelia's life."

"I think I've answered enough questions, and it's time for you to leave."

"I only have one more question, please."

"Go on."

"Do you know of a company named Hailer, LLC in Pensacola?"

"No, I've never heard of it."

"Okay, thank you. That's all for now. If you think of anything else, I am in the area for the next week. Here's my card. If you think of anything at all, no matter how insignificant you think it is, you can reach me any time. Thank you again for helping me with my investigation, and we'll be in touch."

William got up without saying a word and opened the door to see Alphonso out.

Alphonso thought about the meeting as he drove. Even though William was rude and defensive, he seemed genuinely concerned that Amelia is in danger.

Chapter Eighteen

UNANSWERED QUESTIONS

After talking to William, Alphonso had a shocking perspective on him. His sister is kind, business-oriented, and understanding. He's quite the opposite, arrogant and disrespectful. If he knows nothing about the Hailer real estate developer, it could mean that he had no connection with the threats.

Alphonso put the meeting behind him. He'd one more stop-off, and then he's officially on vacation. He concentrated on pleasant thoughts and the anticipation of being with Jocelyn on the beach later. Alphonso imagined how great she'd look in her swimsuit, and it put a smile on his face.

He didn't know how he'd approach this company's owner and would play it by ear depending on his reception. He'd a forty-five-minute drive from William's business.

It surprised him how elegant and beautiful the Hailer office building was from the outside. Inside, the décor was stunning.

He'd asked the administrator if he could speak to the owner. She said he wasn't in the office today, and his wife handled his appointments in his absence. Alphonso admitted he didn't have an appointment but had tried several times to make one. He'd asked to speak to the owner's wife concerning a real estate venture. The administrator dialed her number and said it was okay. She came out to meet him.

"Hello, I am Cadence Small. My husband, Tyler Small, must have forgotten about you being here today. How can I help you?"

"Hi, my name is Alphonso Lott and I am an investigator with Soco & Soco Law firm in Fairbanks, Alaska. Could I have a few minutes of your time, please?"

"Sure, come on down to my office."

"This is a beautiful building."

"Thank you. My father-in-law, who is no longer with us, designed it. And, over the years, we've updated it to keep it current with other businesses in the area."

"I am sorry."

"It's okay. My father-in-law died five years ago."

"Come on in and have a seat. I'll close the door, so we're not disturbed if you don't mind.?"

"Yes, it's okay."

"Now, what brings you here this morning?"

"I'll get right to the point. First, here's my card should you have any need to contact the firm for verification on me."

"You're a long way from home."

"Believe it or not, I'm here on vacation, but it coincided with a case that may involve your company."

"My husband is the best person to talk to, but he's out sick today; I can try to answer your questions."

"Thank you. Our client owns a hotel in Anchorage. Someone approached her to sell it for the buying company to build a live work and play townhome community in its place. We suspect multiple developers are working as a conglomerate company to force her to sell. Are you aware of anything like this?"

"No, I am not. And I don't see what this has to do with our company. However, we have a similar project under contract in Seattle."

"How far from completion is it?"

"I'm not sure, but no demolition has taken place yet. I stay away from the business as much as possible. I'm only here to attend a meeting in my husband's absence."

"Is Hailer in partnership with any other company for your project in Seattle? Or do you know of any collaborations on projects in the past?"

"Not that I am aware of. We are a solo developer with our own portfolio. We hire outside contractors as required and for specific jobs. That's the way my husband's father did it, and he has continued that practice."

"How many people do you employ?"

"We have twenty employees, and we contract most of the work out to another ten regular companies."

"Do you have an office in Alaska.?"

"No, this office handles all our business projects. We've completed some projects in the Alaska area, though. Because of the zoning laws in different states, we try to build in areas with similar regulations as Pensacola."

"Have you heard of someone named William Haley who owns Pensacola's Best Tours?"

"No. William Haley name isn't familiar, but I've heard of the touring company. Pensacola Chamber of Commerce has a Christmas party every year and invites local business owners. I could've met the owner there, I suppose."

"Does your husband have any political connections in Alaska?"

"I don't think he does, but my father-in-law was into politics and had many connections in places that I would never dream of."

"I think you've answered all my questions, Mrs. Small. I can't think of anything else right now. Thank you again for your time and for talking to a stranger."

"You too, thank you, but to be clear, I'm going to verify who you are as soon as you leave."

"I would do the same if an investigator showed up at my business without an appointment. If you think of anything or have questions, call."

"Before you leave, Can I be honest with you, please? It's rather delicate?"

"Go ahead. Anything you say will be in the strictest confidence."

"I don't know if I'm speaking out of turn or even if you are who you say you are. But I'm going to take a chance on you, Mr. Alphonso Lott. My husband has been acting strange. I'm hoping you can figure out what is happening in this company because rumors about illegal actions are rampant amongst the employees. Things have filtered back to me, and I'm concerned. My husband says everything is okay whenever I try to talk to him. I just need to figure out the truth."

"What I can tell you is that a young woman is living in fear of her life. She's receiving death threats. We may find out Hailer, LLC is not involved and can absolve him of all guilt. I promise we are doing everything we can to sort this out, and we'll keep you informed. No need to worry, and don't forget to ring me if you have any concerns or hear anything else. I'll be in touch."

"I will. And thank you so much for coming. Please enjoy the rest of your time here."

"Thank you; I will do my best."

He'd received some helpful information, after all. He'd learned the name of the CEO, and this project in Seattle sounded like the same operation as the Anchorage project. Alphonso suspected that Cadence's husband was lying to her, or at least concealing his business dealings. He'd no reason to doubt her, but she may know William or something about his company. Talking to her had turned out better than talking to her husband.

Chapter Nineteen

REASSURANCE FROM SISTER

After talking to Alphonso, William was concerned about his sister and called her. He'd needed to hear from Amelia for himself that she's okay. William had coordinated with Tyler to get her to sell the hotel, and that deal didn't come through. He'd assumed Tyler had done the same; At least that's what he'd told him. If Tyler was in this and something happened to his sister, he'd never forgive himself.

"Hello, Sis. How are you doing?"

"Hello, William. I'm okay, what about you?"

"I'm better now that I hear your voice."

"It is good to hear from you. You could text now and then to see how the business is going, even though the last time we talked, you got angry," Amelia said.

"You're right, we need to talk more often, and I promise to do better. Now that the tantrum is over. How are things going with the hotel?"

"Since the last time we talked, there have been some threats against my life to force me to sell. You know I'll never sell it. As a precaution, I've moved into the hotel. I was getting threatening letters at the house, on my cell, and in my office at the hotel. I reported everything to the police, and I've hired an attorney to investigate. I also have additional security at the hotel."

"I know all about your pet investigator; he called at my

office this morning. He thinks I've got something to do with it, you know that's not true, right? Can't you keep him on a leash? Seriously though, sis, it sounds bad for you."

"I'm not afraid."

"I know you're not. You are a lot like our dad. He was as stubborn as an ox, too. He would've done anything to protect our family and the hotel. Would it help if I came and stayed with you for a couple of weeks?"

"That's unnecessary. You have your own business to run. There's nothing you can do. Let the police do what the police do best. You can keep in touch more, though. That would make me feel better than anything else."

"I will. Please call if anything else happens, and I'll keep in touch. I love you, Sis."

"Love you, too, and I'm glad my one and only brother called."

Chapter Twenty

VACATION SURPRISE

Alphonso took off his work clothes at the hotel, slipped into his new swimming trunks, and went to find Jocelyn.

He's surprised to find her under a beach umbrella with another man standing beside her having a conversation. Alphonso stood still and watched their reactions to each other for a few minutes. It appeared they knew each other because the guy put his hand on her shoulder. Jocelyn did not say she knew anyone here. The guy looked familiar. As he got closer, he couldn't believe his eyes. Jocelyn was talking to William. What the hell was going on? Suspicious thoughts ran through his mind, and he didn't like what he's seeing. It was clear why William changed the time of their meeting. He'd confronted the problem head-on by walking over and greeting them.

"Hi, Jocelyn. I see you've met someone. How coincidental that we both know your friend." William looked as shocked as Alphonso. He'd stepped away from Jocelyn's beach chair. "Hello, Alphonso. Well, what a small world, how do you two know each other?" William asked.

"It appears you are old friends?" Alphonso said.

Jocelyn didn't get up, but she had the good grace to look flustered. The look of surprise told him she wasn't expecting him back yet and made him think something was going on between them. She looked extremely uncomfortable.

"Care to explain what's going on, Jocelyn," Alphonso asked.

"I was meeting some friends at a restaurant for lunch. They are running late, so I came to the beach," William explained.

William took up the story. "After our meeting this morning, I was walking on the beach and guess, what? I ran into my old friend Jocelyn, who I haven't seen for years."

"Is he the friend you were telling me about?"

"Yes."

"You didn't tell me he still lived here."

"I guess I forgot a few teeny details."

"Don't let me break up a reunion. I have some emails to send back to the office. Why don't I do that, and you can call me when you're free, Jocelyn? Goodbye again, William."

Alphonso stalked back to his room, set up his laptop, and stared at it. What the hell just happened. It made no sense, and the piece didn't fit the puzzle. How can Jocelyn be mixed up with William and be on vacation with him? He'd thought about the reactions from Jason when he mentioned Jocelyn. Jason emphasized Alphonso should not get involved with her. Did he'd just see what Jason had been telling him? Why? Could she and William have something to do with the threats against Amelia and be in it together? Had she played him? This was some vacation.

First, he'd had to work, and now the woman with him might be using him to spend time with an old boyfriend. Unless something changed after this, the vacation was going to be a disaster.

He'd thought about what he learned from his two interviews to focus and figure out where Jocelyn fit into things? He'd believed William knew Tyler and may have worked with him to get his sister to sell. The deal failed. Alphonso doesn't think William had anything to do with the threats to his sister.

How does Jocelyn fit into the picture? She worked at Delta and told him she had an opportunity for management. Was she the connection in Alaska? He couldn't figure out how it helped her with Delta. He'd looked at it from a different angle. Was she in trouble and needed money? What for? He'd emailed his suspicions to Liam to dig and see what they could find out. He waited an hour to give Jocelyn and William time to finish their liaison; she didn't contact him. So, he'd rang her to find out what was going on.

Chapter Twenty-One

DECEPTION DOES NOT WORK

It had been an eventful day for William. First, an interview with Alphonso, and being accused of plotting to harm his sister, and now this situation with Jocelyn. What's next?

"Why didn't you tell me who you came to Pensacola with?" William asked Jocelyn.

"You're blaming me for this? You could've told me who your interview was with today."

"What's going on, J? Didn't you have any intentions of us getting back together again? When I called to meet you here, why didn't you tell me that your new boyfriend could turn up at any second? You're playing games, again. I take it you're just using the investigator to get a free vacation. You mess people up, J. It's easy now to see why our relationship didn't last."

"I wasn't trying to get back with you or use anyone. It was you who called and wanted to see me, remember."

"You could've said, no, but you like having more than one man dangling at a time, don't you? Are you mixed up in this case Alphonso's investigating, is that it? Imagine what the poor bloke's thinking. No wonder he'd looked so shocked when he saw us here. He interviewed me this morning and then found me with his bit of skirt an hour later. What's going on?"

"What case? I know he's investigating something, but he didn't discuss it with me."

"Maybe, I shouldn't say anything, either."

"Who am I going to tell? Talk to me, William."

"Someone has threatened my sister and is trying to force her to sell the hotel."

"Why would they do that?"

William paused, a shadow crossed Jocelyn's face, and he could tell she was hiding something.

"My sister would never sell. Whoever is trying to force her is wasting their time. Listen, J, I'm going to skip lunch if you don't mind. You clearly have other plans and forcing down two lunches with two men is probably not great for your digestion. We've three groups coming in for tours this afternoon. It's good to see you again, but it's probably best if we don't see or call each other again. Enjoy the rest of your vacation."

"Spoilsport. Oh, alright. I suppose I'd ought to go back to the hotel and try to explain to sulky pants how I know you."

"It's going to cause problems."

"With him?" She laughed. "Don't you worry about him; I can handle him. He's a pushover."

If Jocelyn said she'd deal with the situation, William believed her. He'd knew she's good at deception and lying. While driving back to his office, William thought it was always good seeing Jocelyn. He'd liked her unpredictability and the sense of danger being around her. But William was glad they only had a brief relationship. He wouldn't want anything long-term. She's too much drama. When he'd heard she was in town, he asked to see her at the beach. Like most things concerning Jocelyn, it was a terrible idea because she's on vacation with the investigator working on his sister's case. How could he be sure that she wasn't embroiled in it all? It seemed a coincidence that they're all here, and as far as he'd knew,

Jocelyn didn't know Amelia. Jocelyn wasn't the kind of woman you'd take home to meet the family.

Chapter Twenty-Two

DEAL WITH IT

Alphonso wonders what he'd got himself into. This was messy, and if there was one thing he didn't do, it was mixing his work and private life. He could be on vacation with a suspect in his case. That's so messed up. It made his head spin. He'd called Jason to give him an update and get some advice.

"Hello, Jason; this is Alphonso."

"Hello, Alphonso. I didn't expect to hear from you this soon."

"I didn't expect to contact you this soon, either."

"What can I do for you?"

"I have a dilemma. Can you tell me why you react suspiciously every time I mention Jocelyn's name?"

"If I did that, it's an unconscious reaction. I'm concerned about you and hope you find the special lady you're looking for."

"Well, I don't think it's going to be her."

"You've only been away for two days. What's happened?"

"After my interview with Amelia's brother this morning, I found him and Jocelyn on the beach together."

"What do you mean, together."

"Well, they didn't look as though they were talking about the weather, and how on earth do they know each other? Neither of them confessed. It's awkward, but they seemed close. I think they've dated at some point. I might just be the fool that paid for her to get back to her boyfriend."

"Do you think she's that type of person, Alphonso?"

"Right now, I don't know what she's capable of. I think they might both be in on this case. What should I do?"

"Foremost, observe client confidentiality. Don't tell her what you are investigating. Be careful and watch your back. Find out why she met with William. She owes you that explanation. Have you had your meeting with the real-estate developer?"

"Yes, but I only spoke to his wife. She didn't know about a project in Alaska, but they have a similar project in Seattle. The husband was sick and not in the office. It seemed like the lady just wanted somebody to talk to. Her husband's name is Tyler."

"Cut your vacation short and come home. We can arrange for another one soon. I promise, and we understand you've been waiting a long time for this one. But right now, I'm concerned about your safety. Let me know how things go with Jocelyn. I don't want to do it on an open line, but when you get back, I'll explain my concern, and it has nothing to do with the case."

"Well, I wished you'd told me before I left. You could've saved me a lot of time and money. I agree with you about cutting the vacation short. Thank you for being understanding, and I'll talk to you soon. Goodbye, Jason."

As soon as he finished talking to Jason, there's a knock on his door. It was Jocelyn. Was she listening at the door? He let her in.

"I was about to call you to see if you wanted to have lunch; we need to talk. The hotel has a buffet lunch today. Would you like to try it or go out?" Alphonso asked. He could barely look at her, but he'd still had his manners, and although their vacation was probably over, he still wanted to give her choices.

"The hotel is fine. Can you give me five minutes to slip into some slacks?"

"I'll meet you in the restaurant," Alphonso said hesitantly.

The restaurant was overflowing with hotel guests in a beautiful sunroom with a glass enclosure. It's decorated with fresh flowers. There was beach paraphernalia on the walls that gave you a beach-like feel, even though it was raining outside. They ordered a glass of wine each.

"This is a nice spread for lunch. I hope it is as good as it looks. Hotels use the cheapest ingredients and the night before's leftovers to make up their buffets. Then they top it off with fresh fruit and salad and expect people to not notice. It's a rip-off," Jocelyn moaned.

"And how much does it cost you, exactly? Can't you just be grateful for anything?"

Alphonso had snapped at her without meaning to. "I'm sorry. I didn't mean to say that."

"That's okay; I understand that you're angry, and I think we need to clear the air over lunch."

She squeezed his arm, and he'd felt himself relenting. There was a wide variety of seafood, chicken and steak, an assortment of vegetables, salad, and a table filled with desserts. Their wine was on the table when they returned. After a few minutes of trying a little of everything on their plates, Jocelyn was the first to speak.

"This food is great, and I am glad you suggested it."

"It is good."

"About today with William, I can only imagine what you're thinking. I'm on vacation with you, and then you find me on the beach with someone else. I've known William for a long time, and we had a brief relationship. I haven't talked to him in years. But I called him to say hi. I didn't even expect him to have the same phone number."

"And you think that's an okay thing to do when you're on vacation at someone else's expense."

"That's twice you've mentioned money, is that all you care about? Look, Alphonso, it was nothing. He'd insisted he come by and say hello after his interview. I didn't know that the meeting was with you. I didn't think he'd still be here when you got back."

"I bet you didn't."

"Oh, Alphonso. Stop sulking, baby. You sound like a little boy.

I apologize for everything that happened today."

"I know it appears that I'm disrespectful. I did not know it was William at first, and then he'd turned to face you as I was approaching, and I realized who it was. I was angry and felt used. I will accept your apology and explanation. Is there anything else you want to tell me about this relationship with William or anything else connected with him?"

She smiled at him, but it wasn't convincing.

"No, I've told you everything. Is there something I need to know about the interview you had with William? Is he in trouble?"

"No, he's not in trouble."

"But you said you were working a case."

"Well, I am, and it involves someone he knows, and that's all I'm prepared to say about it. Under the circumstances, I think we should get an early flight back to Alaska."

"Oh no, Fonzie. Come on, we can put this behind us and still have a lovely time together, can't we?" She pouted and shifted her position to show off more of her shapely legs.

"Don't call me that again. I prefer you to use my given name, Alphonso. The flight back is scheduled for Saturday, but I would like to get an early flight out on Friday morning."

Chapter Twenty-Three

WHAT'S NEXT

Alphonso was upset with Jocelyn. She made him look like a fool in front of William. After everything he'd done to please her, she was disrespectful. As for as he's concerned, the vacation was over. She's right about one thing, he's behaving like a child, but he'd felt deeply hurt and betrayed. He can't see how they can pull this back and enjoy the rest of their time together. He'd absorbed himself in a shower and came up with an idea of how to fix this mess.

He's having second thoughts about Jocelyn and William being involved in the threats, though, so if he's right, that's one good thing to come of all this. It would delight Amelia to find out that her brother wasn't behind this. But how did Jocelyn benefit from the case? When they had dinner that evening, he'd try to get more information about her relationship with William.

He called Liam to let him know he'd be back sooner than planned.

"Hello, man, this is Alphonso."

"Yes, I have your number on my phone, you know. You must not be having a good time if you're calling me. What's up?"

"There's been a hiccup, and I'm trying to figure it out. The reason for my call is to let you know I'll be back on Friday instead of Saturday."

"Why are you cutting your vacation short?"

"I found out my companion on this trip could be a suspect in our case."

"Wait just a minute. You've a woman with you on this trip, and you think she's involved in our case. No one in the office knew you were dating because all you do is work. Give me more information about your vacation partner."

"There's not a lot to tell. She's a Delta airline attendant and someone I met at the airport in Fairbanks. I've known her for about three years. This is our second date. When I met Jocelyn, is irrelevant right now? But I need your advice."

"So, you've known a woman for three years, and this is only your second date?"

"I'll tell you all about it when I get back to the office."

"I can hardly wait."

"William is no longer a suspect in this case, based on the interview I had with him this morning. It surprised him that this had been happening to his sister, and I believe him. This's where it gets crazy. At some point, my date had a relationship with William. My vacation is a disaster."

"Alphonso, you need to be careful. From what you are telling me, something is not adding up."

"I met the real estate developer's wife, Cadence, and not him. I need you to do a couple of things for me without the brothers' knowledge. Look into Jocelyn and Cadence's backgrounds and see what you can find. You need to look into who is buying all the condos in my community. This could also be related to our case. I should be in the office on Monday morning."

"There have been no threats to Amelia since you left. But we're following up some leads and working with the police."

"Okay, Liam, if anything else comes up here, I'll call. I brought Jason up to speed earlier, so you don't have to brief him. He thought I should come home right away. So, I'll keep you posted."

"Do what Jason suggested; We need you back home and safe."

After his call with Liam, Alphonso changed their flight schedules with no problem. With work to do, he put together an information paper about what had happened in his interviews, then submitted it to Jason and Liam.

He'd searched the internet for directions to a recommended restaurant for dinner. Then, with the TV on, he'd dosed and got a couple of hours of sleep.

A loud noise outside woke him. Some children were playing in the hallway, probably because of the rain, and bumped his door. They apologized and ran down the hall. He didn't know why their parents allowed them to roam the hotel, where everybody is a stranger. After he'd washed his face, he bit the bullet and called Jocelyn.

"Hello, it's me."

"Hi. I've been waiting for you to get in touch. It's been a while since lunch, and I'm hungry. Are you ready to take me out for dinner?" Jocelyn asked.

"Yes, I am. I had a nap, and I'm ready to eat, as well."

"What time will you be ready?"

"What about twenty minutes?"

"Okay, please come and get me as soon as you are ready," said Jocelyn. "Oh, what should I wear?"

"It is casual, nothing dressy."

"Okay."

They prepared for dinner in their separate rooms. After twenty minutes, despite asking Alphonso to get her, there was a knock on his door.

"It's me, and I'm ready."

"Okay." As soon as he saw her, every bad thought he had melted away.

"Wow, you look beautiful."

"Thank you.   when the dress is casual. What are we eating this evening?"

"We're going to the Flounders Chowder House. It's owned by three brothers and has a recorded history of a large marlin and a human-sized eating clam inside the restaurant. They've inside and outside seating, and it will be an experience for us. They serve flounder cooked in a variety of recipes, other seafood, and my favorite dessert, key lime pie."

"Another chowder house, though. I thought you might've chosen something different tonight. But I'm starving, so let's go."

While giving the description of the restaurant, his mood lifted. Jocelyn's criticism of his restaurant choice on top of everything else annoyed him, but he ignored it.

"It sounds like an exciting place and a relaxed atmosphere."

"Before we get there, can you please tell me the truth about your relationship with William?"

"The last few years of my marriage weren't great. My husband and I made the mistake of reaching out to other people instead of working through our problems together. I met William one night while I was out having a drink. He'd said it looked like I was carrying the weight of the world on my shoulders. He was half right. I was carrying a weight of uncertainty about my marriage and didn't know what to do."

"So, he'd picked you up in a bar?"

"Well, yes, but it wasn't as sordid as your tone suggests. I gave William my number, and our relationship started the next day. We went out on several dates and had a lot of fun, but it didn't last because of my marital status. Before you say it, yes. I did cheat on my husband, and there's no excuse for doing that. But I found out he was doing the same thing. We both had several affairs, but he died before we could reconcile. My husband and I had a daughter who is now six years old."

"You didn't even think I'm important enough to tell me you've a daughter, and you were married."

"I didn't know where this relationship was going any more than you did. I wouldn't bring my daughter into a relationship five minutes after it starts."

"Now I understand why you told me you'd let me know the next day whether you could come on this trip. It wasn't about the job, but coordination with your mother to babysit."

"Yes, that is partially true, but I had vacation time due at work, so being away wasn't an issue."

"Is it also probably true, the first date we went on that your mother was at the movie with your daughter and not out alone or with friends?"

"Yes, Alphonso."

"What else? Why this reunion with William?"

"Until today, I didn't know that he still had feelings for me, even though we weren't together long. We kept each other's numbers."

"Have you met William's sister?"

"I knew he had a sister because he'd talked about her a lot, but I've never met her."

"Did he tell you why we were meeting today?"

"He said a little but seemed concerned about his sister's safety and that she might lose the hotel. He didn't go into detail."

"Did you know I was working on a case concerning his sister before we came on this trip?"

"No, I didn't."

"Why do I feel as though you're lying to me?"

"I'm telling the truth. I don't know what else I can say."

Jocelyn looked emotional and almost in tears.

"I'm sorry if I've upset you, but I am an investigator, and I need to know that you're telling me the truth. Up until now, you lied or didn't disclose some important facts about yourself."

"I understand, and this is all my fault, but you're coming at me so hard about this, and there's nowhere for me to go, so I'm a little emotional."

"Now that I understand why you met with William, it was best we had this conversation before dinner. I feel better, and I hope we can have a good evening out. Let's make the best of it and try to put it behind us for the rest of tonight, at least."

"I hope we can. Thank you, Alphonso."

"We're at the restaurant. It looks like a nice place."

"I agree with you. I'd like to go to the restroom before being seated if you don't mind."

"No, I don't mind at all."

When Jocelyn returned from the restroom, Alphonso had a glass of wine waiting for her before looking at the menu.

"This is an incredibly unique restaurant, but I like it. They have areas for children to hang out. If a man wanted to buy a lady a present after their meal, there's a gift shop. There's something for everyone," Jocelyn said.

Alphonso couldn't believe she's suggesting he'd buy her a gift after all that had been revealed to him in the last thirty minutes.

"Did you see the giant clam on the wall as we passed by the bar?"

"Yes, I did, but let's look at the menu before the server returns."

"What looks good to you?" Jocelyn had regained her composure, and it felt almost like it did on their first night together. However, the tension between them had only subsided for a moment.

"I'm doing everything, flounder. For an appetizer, I'm going with the flounder's shrimp and spinach dip, then the flounder's chowder to see how it compares to Alaska's chowder." She had an appetite, that was for sure. "No one has chowder like Alaska's."

"We are about to find out. For my entrée, I'm trying the Classic

Stuffed flounder and topping it all off with key lime pie," Alphonso said with a smile.

"I have learned one thing about you, and that is you love key lime pie. Is that the major reason we came here?"

"No. The description of the restaurant intrigued me, and the pie." They both laughed.

"I am going to join you and get the flounder chowder; the red snapper sounds good as an entrée. And since you love key lime pie, I'll try it for the first time."

"Jocelyn, are you telling me you never eaten key lime pie?"

"Absolutely. So, we'll be having a historic moment in Florida together." They both laughed again.

The food was better than they'd hoped it would be. Both desserts arrived soon after they completed the main course.

Alphonso said with a smile, "This key lime is the best I've ever had. I plan on making a special trip every year to come and get some."

"Will you be traveling alone?"

"That remains to be seen." She was back to her flirty ways; it seemed she couldn't help herself.

"I'm surprised at how tasty the dessert was. But nothing can compare with Alaskan chowder, even though this one was delicious."

"I'm glad you've enjoyed everything. I don't know if you've heard of the Broken Egg café, but I thought we could have breakfast there tomorrow morning."

"No, I hadn't heard of it."

"That'll be another first for us together. What time would you like to get out in the morning."

"What about nine a.m."

"That's great. You sure you don't want to sleep late?"

"No, I want to enjoy the days we've left as much as possible before going home on Friday."

He glanced in the gift window shop on the way to get the car and noticed it was a designer jewelry shop. Alphonso carried on walking and ignored her hint from earlier. He might be a gentleman, but he wasn't a fool. They were quiet in the car for the short ride to the hotel until the last five minutes.

"Thank you for a wonderful evening and for being understanding, Alphonso."

"No problem."

"Do we have plans after breakfast? I believe it's a significant area to go shopping?"

"I've never been to Pensacola, so I thought we'd take a guided tour of the city. Initially, I'd planned to ask William, but it isn't a good idea given what happened today. I've booked with another company. I apologize for not asking you what you wanted to do."

"No problem. After the tour, the only thing I want to do is to check out a mall and do some shopping. I can't go home without souvenirs for my mother and daughter."

"Okay. Our tour tomorrow is for two hours and starts at 1:00 p.m. We'll have time afterward to shop, and maybe the tour guide can recommend a place to eat dinner as well."

They arrived back at the hotel and went to their separate rooms.

Chapter Twenty-Four

TIME AT BEACH

On Wednesday morning, Alphonso woke up with unanswered questions and suspicious thoughts on his mind. He opened the curtains to a beautiful view of the Pensacola beach from his window. The vacation was supposed to be full of fun, exploring a city and all it offered. Learning about Jocelyn and determining if she would be a good fit for a soulmate had taken a backseat. Alphonso was wrapped in a cloud of uncertainty. He made a cup of coffee and hoped he'd feel better for it. He guessed his lucky Bombas socks would not have helped him, even if he had packed them.

It made no sense that he came all this way and not even enjoyed the beach. He put on his swimming trunks, grabbed a towel, and headed down there. Some alone time was probably for the best. He found the perfect spot and put his towel on one of the hotel's beach chairs to enjoy the view before taking a swim. The water was cold because it was early in the morning, but once he had been in for a few minutes and had his muscles pumping in a steady rhythmic front-crawl, it felt warmer. Being on the beach was what he had needed for the last two years, complete relaxation, with nothing on his mind but enjoying his time alone.

He came out of the water to see Jocelyn sitting on a towel next to his. She was wearing a black two-piece swimsuit, and man, did she look good. She could make a man forget any wrongs she'd done him.

"Alphonso, it's me. You looked a little startled."

"Sorry, the sun was in my eyes, and I wasn't sure it was you. My, you look beautiful in your swimsuit. So, you woke up early, as well. You should have called me."

"I didn't want to wake you. I figured since we have a planned day out later, that I'd get a quick dip in the ocean before we head out to breakfast."

"It would've been okay; I was awake, and I feel like a little kid this morning; I looked out the window and saw how beautiful the ocean looked and couldn't resist."

"It's nice out this morning, not too hot, yet just enough chill in the air for a good swim."

"My daughter wanted to talk to me this morning, so I was awake early. My mother said she refused to go to school until she heard my voice. I miss her as much as she misses me. Children do that to you, but I've no complaints. Her name is Mia, and she's the best thing that's ever happened to me. I love her very much."

Alphonso swallowed the feeling of resentment and forced a smile. Jocelyn purposefully hid the existence of Mia from him, and now it seemed she had plenty to say about her. Alphonso wouldn't have judged her for having a child. We all had a past, but he'd resented Jocelyn for not being honest with him.

"I can tell you love her by your expression and how you speak about her with such affection. I hope to have that feeling myself one day."

"It's a shame that you've never married and had children of your own. I think you'd make an excellent father."

"Over the years, work has impeded any relationship, but starting this year, I will not let my personal life suffer."

"Well, I'm not one to advise about marriage, but I can tell you great things about being a parent. Even though sometimes it's not a simple job,

I wouldn't change it for the world."

"Do you fancy swimming together?" Alphonso suggested.

"Yes, I'd love to." They swam and experimented with each other until they had enough.

"I guess we should get back to the hotel so we can continue our plans for today, starting with breakfast. How long will it take you to get ready?"

"Should only take about thirty minutes. I'll knock on your door when I'm ready."

"Sounds good. See you then, Jocelyn."

They left the hotel and arrived at Broken Egg café. Because it was early for vacationers, there was no crowd, and they had their choice of seating. Jocelyn had the lobster and brie omelet, and Alphonso chose the shrimp and grits. They shared a pitcher of delicious cranberry mimosa. The conversation was limited to questions about her.

"Alphonso, this is nutritious food and another excellent choice for a restaurant, but I feel uncomfortable because you are just asking me so many questions this morning. I thought you had forgiven me."

"I don't recall you asking."

"Well, I'm asking now. Will you forgive me?"

"I'm sorry, but this vacation has differed from what I expected. I'm not trying to make you feel uncomfortable or guilty."

"Would you feel better if we didn't go on the tour and go back to the hotel instead?"

"No, it's nonrefundable, and I want to see more of the area."

"If all you're concerned about is the money, I'll pay my portion of the tour."

"There's no reason to get upset. If money was an issue, it wouldn't be an all-expense-paid trip for you. You don't understand the position you have put me in from a legal perspective. If you're involved in my case somehow or know someone that is, there is a conflict of interest in bringing you on vacation. I could lose my license."

"You sound angrier than me. I don't even know what your case involves, and I'm not part of whatever it is you're investigating. So, where does the legal issue come into play? I'm sorry you walked up on William and me at the beach. I can only imagine how that looked. However, it will not be a good day if you're going to suspect me all the time."

"We sound like a couple having their first fight, and it's just a misunderstanding. We will have a good day; I don't want to be miserable or fighting any more than you do. Since we had a late breakfast, it's almost time for our tour. Let's enjoy it. I promise I'm okay if you are." Alphonso paid for the meal and left a generous tip.

Chapter Twenty-Five

HIS GUARD IS UP

Knowing that Jocelyn had an affair and had a child was a surprise to Alphonso, but he still wanted to know her. Maybe they could salvage the vacation, and he could enjoy the last two days.

They arrived at the tour fifteen minutes before leaving and made small talk with other tourists. He'd sensed negative vibes from her but decided that he would enjoy his day and wouldn't let Jocelyn spoil it for him.

This tour comprised a small group of six people, so he'd expected it to be personal and educational. He had prepaid for the tickets, so they were seated on the bus immediately.

"Jocelyn, I want to forget about what happened in the last couple of days and enjoy this tour and shopping with you later."

"You're right. We are adults, so we can move on and have a nice day. Thank you for coordinating the tour, and I'm looking forward to doing some shopping."

"To be honest with you, marriage is on my radar, and I am ready to settle down and have a family. But I'm surprised and disappointed with the way things have gone on this trip. There are certain things that you should have told me before."

"Oh, so this vacation was just an interview for you to find a potential mate." They both laughed.

"You have a beautiful smile."

"Thank you."

The Tour guide interrupted their conversation with information about their first stop. They would make five stops, with thirty minutes at each.

They would have enough time to take pictures, visit the gift shops, and stop at an ice cream parlor on the way out.

This tour was great because it gave them a perspective on the city's history. But the highlight of the day was the last stop at the Old City Market, a place that reminded Alphonso of the ice cream shops you saw in classic movies. They had the root beer floats, something you would never find in Alaska.

"I enjoyed myself today. The first time I came here, I didn't tour the city. Today was educational, fun, and climaxed with delicious ice cream I've never had before. What could be better, Alphonso?"

"I'm glad you enjoyed yourself. This is the first time we have laughed together since we got here. The guide gave us some excellent suggestions for shopping. As soon as we get back to the car, we can get started on the second leg of our day, and the third will be dinner. What would you like to eat after we finish shopping?"

"I'm not sure. After we've checked out every store in the mall and found some pleasant things for myself and my two special girls, I'll be starving." Alphonso noticed that she'd added gifts for herself to the shopping list but hadn't thought to include him.

"I thought you said you only have one child?"

"The other girl is my mother. She acts like a kid sometimes when she's with my daughter."

"Oh. I see. The tour guide says we should go to Cordova Mall. It's the largest in the city and upscale."

"Sounds good."

"And I'd like you to select where we eat tonight? I want you to enjoy yourself." Alphonso was doing his best to placate her.

"Okay. While you were in the bathroom, I heard another couple talking about a restaurant named Jaco's Bayfront Bar and Grill on Palafox street. It's a local favorite and has a variety of items on the menu that we like. It is also a causal dress restaurant, so we don't have to go back to the hotel to change clothes and come back out. It overlooks Palafox pier Marina so the views should be magnificent. I'll google the mall and restaurant. The couple in front of us said that Palafox Street is a gateway to downtown Pensacola. It was once one of the ten best streets in America. Along the southern end, there are lots of shops, dining opportunities, and boutiques."

"Sounds like we should go there to shop for souvenirs, as well."

"I want to compare Pensacola mall to ours in Alaska. Let's go to the mall first and Palafox shopping after we finish eating dinner. The shops are open late, or if it gets too late, we can always come back tomorrow."

"Wow, you really like shopping, huh?"

After leaving the tour bus and swapping it for the car, Jocelyn found directions for the mall and restaurant.'

"We're in luck. The restaurant is only fifteen minutes from the mall. We'll have lots of time in the mall."

"I figured we'll be at the mall for a minimum of five hours."

"No, I mostly shop for my daughter, but I'm hoping to find some pleasant things for me, as well. We should be ready to head for dinner around six-thirty."

"We shall see."

"You are about to learn something about me. Not every woman wants to hang out at the mall for hours and hours. I know what I like and have a nose for finding the best shops."

After getting to the mall, Jocelyn suggested they went in separate directions and meet back up at the entrance at six p.m. She made all the correct protests and said, 'Are you sure?' more than once, but Alphonso found himself parted from another three hundred of his hard-earned dollars. He wanted her to be happy, and seeing her face lit up in lively excitement made it all worth it.

Now, back in the car and headed to the restaurant, traffic is heavy and limits their conversation on the way to dinner. They arrive within twenty-five minutes, and Jocelyn was texting and receiving a text from someone the entire time.

"Is something wrong?" Alphonso asked.

"No, why do you ask?"

"I just noticed the expressions on your face while you were texting. One minute you are smiling, then you looked angry or disappointed. I thought maybe something might be going on with your mother or daughter."

"No, just a friend I had not talked to in a long time. Am I annoying you? If so, I will call them when we get back to the hotel?"

"No, I'm fine. Just surprised you were doing a lot of texting and not said one word to your vacation buddy."

"Do I detect a little jealousy?"

"No, as I said, I'm okay. Oh, we're at the restaurant."

As they entered the restaurant, they found it was more extensive on the inside than it looked from the street. All seating had a window view of the marina.

Sailboats bobbed on the ocean in front of them, and the water sprinkled with a million shining diamonds of light. The marina was chock with moored yachts, and, as if they'd ordered it, the sun set as their wine arrived, and they sat in an orange glow of descending sunlight sipping on the dry white.

"This is a unique place you selected, Jocelyn." Alphonso compliments her on her excellent taste.

"I'm glad you approve. Let's see what's on the menu the server gave us. These are some of the weirdest names for drinks I have ever heard of. I'm normally a one or two glass wine drinker, but I'll be adventurous tonight and try the grapefruit basil smash."

"That's a coincidence; I was thinking about having the same thing. The seafood stew looks like it will be good, as well. I am going to have that for my entrée."

"You know what? I think I'll have the same. That's scary. The same drinks, now the same entrees. And, they have key lime pie, so I'm having that for dessert."

"That's not scary at all, Alphonso. Our taste in food and drink is similar, it shows we are very compatible. I'm going to have the drunken berries for dessert, though. Just to be different and to avoid freaking you out."

Alphonso wonders if that's the only thing they have in common.

The server returns for their orders and tells them about the pod of dolphins that follow the fishing boats back into the harbor at sunset. The hostess said if they were lucky, they might see them tonight. Five minutes later, sure enough, they saw half a dozen dolphins jumping along in the surf and silhouetted by the setting sun. By the stunned look on his face, it's the most beautiful thing Alphonso had ever seen. He'd wished he was watching the amazing sight with the love of his life.

"Tomorrow is our last day here; I would like to spend time at the beach unless you have other plans," Alphonso suggested.

"That's fine with me. I was thinking the same thing. It's a great idea. Do you want to get out early?"

"Around ten or ten-thirty, maybe? We can have an early breakfast at the hotel and lunch on the beach, and we can decide later what we want to do for the afternoon and dinner."

"I like it. Since we haven't had dinner at the hotel, why don't we eat there tomorrow night?" Jocelyn pointed out.

"Sounds good to me. That will give us time to pack and rest before our long day of travel on Friday."

The server returned with their drinks and entrée. They finished their meal, but the day wasn't over yet. Next, they headed to Palafox street for more shopping.

"We haven't been in the hotel bar since the first night, before going to our rooms. Would you like to have a glass of wine with me?"

"No, not tonight. We've had a long day. I'm tired. I just want to take a shower and go to bed," Jocelyn said.

"Okay. You are right; we have had a long day."

Jocelyn wanted to get to her room. She made calls to her mother and then to a friend. She knew Mia would be in bed, so she chatted to her mom instead. Ava asked a million questions about why they were ending the vacation early. Jocelyn said she'd explain when they get home.

The second call was to a friend in Anchorage, whom she had been texting at dinner. She told him she'd be home late Friday evening, and he needed to follow through with their plan before Monday and make sure there were no witnesses. After her two calls, she watched TV then went to bed.

Chapter Twenty-Six

VACATION LAST DAY

Alphonso wanted to sleep for a couple more hours, but he's glad he set the alarm to have breakfast with Jocelyn that morning. He'd looked forward to this vacation for years, and nothing turned out the way he'd thought it would. He wasn't as green as she thought and still believed that Jocelyn was up in the case somehow. The coincidence was too incredible for her not to be. The only thing that annoyed him yesterday was she was constantly texting someone and became upset with him when he'd asked her about it. Alphonso didn't trust her and thought he could get more out of her before going their separate ways. He'd thought she would slip up after the encounter on the beach with William, but she was nice most of the day yesterday. Alphonso made the best of it and enjoyed his day, and indeed her company, but he would not let his guard down. He wondered if there was any connection between her and Hailer's real-estate company.

Washing your face and brushing your teeth on waking up was like the first snow of the season in Alaska. You know it's coming and what you need to do, but it doesn't make getting out of a warm bed any more pleasant. He'd ring Jocelyn now that he's awake and had fresh breath.

"Hello. Are you calling to see if I'm ready for breakfast?"

"Yes, but first, I want to know how you slept last night?" Alphonso asked.

"I slept like a baby in this enormous room all alone. What about you?"

"I watched TV for a couple of hours, but I slept well in my suite. What time would you like to eat?"

"Would eight-thirty be, okay?"

"Yes. Do you want me to wait for you, or do you want to meet in the hotel restaurant?"

"I will meet you there, Alphonso."

"Okay. See you in a few minutes."

Alphonso guessed he would get through one more day of pretense. It wasn't supposed to be this way, but at least he'd got away from work a few days.

He'd put his swimming trunks on with a t-shirt, so he didn't have to come back to the room before going to the beach. Alphonso wondered if Jocelyn was thinking about him. She messed up with the incident at the beach with William when it could have been different for them. He gave thanks. He saw what she's like in good time and felt that he'd had a lucky escape. How many women get to go on an all-expense-paid vacation after going on one date? Few, he would guess.

As he saw Jocelyn walk into the restaurant, he motioned her to where he was sitting. Man, she always looked good, no matter what time of day it was. He's accepted that their relationship was not meant to be. He'd make the best of his last day with her because he wouldn't be calling for any more dates after they returned home.

"Good morning. You look beautiful and refreshed this morning. But, of course, you always look great."

"Good morning to you and thank you for the compliment. I see we had the same thing on our minds this morning. You are in your swim trunks and are ready to dive."

"I want us to enjoy every minute of today out of our rooms. So, we can go straight to the beach and enjoy it."

"I guess we have no choice but to eat at the buffet because that's all they serve, and it's probably less work for the staff who prepare it and hope you give them a tip."

"Are you ready to see what's waiting for us on the buffet, then?" Alphonso was irritated again. His efforts were never good enough for her. No doubt she wanted to eat breakfast at an expensive restaurant on the seafront. He'd bit back a sarcastic retort and smiled; the last thing he wanted to do was argue with her.

"I am ready. Lead the way."

"The weather report said we may get some rain around four this afternoon. Our plan to hang at the beach, have lunch there, and dinner at the hotel may have worked out to our benefit." Alphonso tried to keep the conversation light.

"I called my mother, got into bed, and didn't see any news last night. I hope there's no rain forecast for tomorrow while we are traveling."

"Hopefully, it's going to be a beautiful day."

"I'm glad it's not a huge airport that we fly out of tomorrow. I hate enormous crowds with everyone bumping into each other. And you always get that one family of people running because they are late for their flights, children running wild, and everyone talks so loud with their ear pods in."

Moan, moan, moan. "I thought you loved flying from different airports. I love flying and wished I could take more vacations, but I don't like disrespectful travelers."

"You are lucky. I work at the airport and rarely get to fly. That's why I wanted to come on this trip with you. I needed to get away from the chaos."

"I'm going to enjoy the food this morning because you know we never get a seafood buffet of this caliber in Alaska," Alphonso said.

"Yes, it's okay; it's still only a buffet, though. I prefer getting a personal table service and high-end produce."

"This is a beautiful place, and I hope to come back someday. Pensacola would be a good place to retire when I've had enough of investigating. What about you? Would you come back here?" Alphonso was digging and hoped she'll let something else slip.

"Yes, I would, but I plan to be in Hawaii this time next year. I have always dreamed of living there with my daughter."

"How does your mother feel about that?"

"I have already broken the news to her, and she's not happy about me moving her only granddaughter to a place where we don't know anyone. But she understood that I'm an adult who has a right to make my own decisions about our future. She also knows I was hesitant about moving in with her when my husband died, but I have no regrets. It's going to hurt my daughter initially because she and my mother have a great relationship, but she'll get used to it. Sometimes, Alphonso, we have to disappoint the ones we love for our personal happiness and career development."

"What is special about Hawaii, and why next year?"

"They have all those beaches and the beautiful white sand. And they come up in the statistics as being the most health-conscious state. For two years running, they were voted as the United States' healthiest people by the American Heart Association. It is also time for my daughter and me to be on our own. We've depended on my mother for too long. I'm in line for a promotion into management, and by making this move, we'll have more money to get started."

She complains about not making enough money in her current role. Alphonso wondered where she was getting the extra money to move to her new life. It must be a tidy sum.

"How's the food," Alphonso asks.

"It's great, but I'm ready to go to the beach. I have been to the buffet twice and can't fit any more food in."

Not bad for somebody that doesn't enjoy slumming it on a hotel buffet. "I had my share, as well. As soon as the server brings the check, we can be on our way to the beach for the last time before leaving tomorrow."

"They crowded the beach this morning, Alphonso. I think a lot more people got out before the rain comes. Let's find a suitable spot."

"It could be a reason the hotel is always full because of all the amenities it has. Even though their accommodation is expensive, you get a lot for your money."

My money being the operative words, he thought. "I don't know what you paid for the room, but I agree they include a lot to make you want to come back."

"When I was planning this trip, the vacation planner I worked with gave me some good prices on renting a townhouse on the beach. I wanted to experience the hotel first. But it would be a good idea for a second trip. Anyway, Jocelyn, are you ready to jump in?"

"Yes, and I think I can beat you getting to the water."

"You think so, with all that food in your stomach?"

"Yes."

"That burst of cold when you first hit the water is a shock to your body. I guess it's better than tiptoeing in a little at a time, as some people do. Like ripping off a Band-Aid," Alphonso said.

"Believe it or not, I am one of those people that put my feet in first and slowly sit down in the water until I feel comfortable, putting my body in," Jocelyn replied.

"Who would have thought that. The way you just jumped in?"

"I am extremely competitive. I don't enjoy losing."

"That is a surprise. I had to race you to the ocean before I can learn anything about you."

"What do you need to know?" Jocelyn says in a negative tone.

"I did not mean it as it sounded. But we got off to a suspicious start the first full day we were here. It's normal to learn about people that you don't interact with every day." He replied, trying to avoid another confrontation. She clammed up and stopped talking. This was his last day to find out anything that might be useful.

"You are right. I didn't mean for my voice to come across the way it did, either. I don't want to go back to discussing William. Is that okay with you? Why don't we stick to our plan and take a few laps in the ocean and get some sun in, so my friends back in Alaska can see I got a tan from hanging out at the beach?" She still had a negative tone when she spoke to him.

"I agree, Jocelyn. Let's enjoy the rest of the day. I want to lie out in the sun after our swim and get a tan. For me, since my skin is already a brown tone, it won't take much doing."

"But for me, it will be a significant improvement since my skin is fair."

"Hope you brought suntan lotion because I forgot mine," he confessed.

"Yes, I did. It's another thing the hotel provides in the room. It was under the sink in the bathroom. I haven't had to touch my own."

"That's probably, why I didn't see it. Men are not as observant as women."

"This is one time I agree with you. Now that we've finished our swim, would you mind putting some of that tanning lotion on me?" asked Jocelyn.

"Of course, we have to make the best of these free chairs while we are relaxing on the beach." Jocelyn handed him the lotion and turned onto her front.

"That would be great because it is hard for anyone to put lotion on their own back unless their arms are six feet long. Since your arms are not quite that long, I guess I can help. Thank you so much for today, Jocelyn. It's a beautiful day, and what I pictured my vacation would be like on the beach. Look at the children running wild, and parents telling them not to get too close to the water. There are teenagers on their cell phones instead of enjoying the beach. Lovers walk hand in hand, and we are just here enjoying the beach and having fun away from work." Alphonso felt relaxed in one sense, but he was still alert and looking for any opportunity to draw her out and get her talking about herself.

"I think you've summed it up, except you haven't mentioned the lifeguards who are here to ensure no one has an accident, swimmers, and non-swimmers."

"Yes, they are the most important people on the beach. I feel safer knowing they're there."

"It's almost one. After all that swimming, I could eat some more food. Would you like to get some lunch?" he asked.

"Yes, I'd love to, after we let our suntan lotion hang on for another fifteen minutes."

"Let's try the 'CRABS' restaurant on the beach. I've seen a line outside every day, but there isn't one there today. It must be a sign. The long lines must mean the food is good and not just convenient for beachgoers," Alphonso suggested.

"You know I love seafood, so I'm willing to try it, and it's convenient for us." They both laughed.

"I'm ready if you are. By the way, your tan looks good and will look even better tomorrow," Alphonso said.

"Thank you. Yours don't look too bad, either."

The server asked if they would like inside or outside seating.

"We'll have inside seating facing the beach if possible." Alphonso requested.

"This is a beautiful view of the Gulf of Mexico. Hard to believe we just finished swimming in it. Look at that freshwater tank of fish. The beautiful fish must intrigue children coming in. I know my daughter would be." Jocelyn has a wistful look for a moment, but it did not convince Alphonso.

"It's a better view than I expected from upstairs. It has an ocean breeze coming at you from outside— and a huge crab looking at you when you walk up to the restaurant's entrance. The fish tank filled with beautiful fish makes it perfect. On the first floor, I saw a gift shop, and a band is playing the drums, a crab bar, a play area for children, and customers seated under beach umbrellas waiting to be served. What a great place for lunch," Alphonso said.

"I agree," she replied.

"Let's get a couple of pictures before we leave here. It seems like this may be the highlight of our trip,"

"Being an investigator, I am surprised you would want to have your picture taken."

"I'm also a solver of cases and need evidence to show my colleagues at work that I went on vacation. They think I'm at home pretending to be away."

"Why would they think that?" she asked.

"They know I work all the time and never take time off."

"Is that what Jason demands of his employees?"

"How do you know, Jason?"

"You have mentioned him several times since we've been here."

"I don't recall." Alphonso knew he hadn't mentioned Jason at all. He never talked about his colleagues by name. "You sound as though you know him personally." Alphonso had her and wasn't letting her wriggle out of this one.

"No, I don't. In the state of Alaska, your firm is well known, so maybe I saw his name on the news or online," she replied.

"That's possible, I suppose."

It was possible, but everything sounded suspicious coming from Jocelyn. Her familiarity with his employer reminded him of Jason's reactions whenever he mentioned Jocelyn's name. *Here go my suspicions again.* Alphonso knew something was going on between them; he could feel it. *He would find out when he's back in the office.*

"Let's look at the menu and talk later. What looks good to you?" Alphonso asked.

"Everything looks wonderful to me. But I think I'll have the crab gumbo for an appetizer, an entrée of snow crab & shrimp boil, lemon sorbet for dessert, and crab attack to drink. What about you?"

"You want three courses for lunch, too. Oh, okay then. Why not? I normally eat a lighter lunch, but we are on vacation, I suppose. I'll have a Caesar salad as an appetizer. For entrée, the king combo sounds great. It comprises a king crab, a Dungeness cluster, and a snow crab cluster. And if we're going the whole hog on our last day, I'll do another key lime pie for dessert and a glass of Pinot Grigio."

"I knew you were going to have your favorite dessert. You don't tire of eating it," Jocelyn said.

"You think you know something about me, and no, I don't tire of it."

"Only that anyone who has a couple of meals with you know, your favorite dessert. I don't think that means I know anything about you."

"Did I say something wrong, again?" he asked.

"No, why do you ask?"

"You have that tone of voice again. I thought we could at least get through lunch with no problems." Alphonso said.

"Maybe I need to record myself because I don't understand when you say I have had a change in my tone."

He was glad the server came for their orders because he was ready to return to the room to have lunch alone. Everything he said was wrong, and he couldn't do anything to please Jocelyn. How did he make such a mistake with this woman? But that's why it's called dating, so you can get to know people.

"How old did you say your daughter is?"

"She's six, going on twenty-five."

"And what nice or fun things do you do together?" he asked.

"The park is her favorite place, and she loves to experience fresh foods, so we eat out a lot. She spends most of her time with her grandmother because of the hours I work," she explained.

"How will you handle that once you move to Hawaii?"

"My hours will be the same as her school hours, and I won't have to work weekends."

"It seems like you have everything worked out for your move."

"Not quite. Why the third degree?" Jocelyn asked.

"No third degree, just trying to make conversation. I figured that if we talked about your daughter, you wouldn't get upset with me. But I was wrong on that score, as well. I am not sure what button I have pushed. Please accept my apology," Alphonso requested.

"I feel you are investigating me since I said something about your employer."

"Should I be investigating you?" asked Alphonso.

"No, it was just a misunderstanding. Can you excuse me for a minute? I need to go to the restroom."

"Sure. Do you know where it is?"

"No, of course, I don't. I've never been here before. But I can ask the server."

Oh no, Alphonso didn't want her stepping away. He had her rattled, and she might have said something in temper that she may regret later.

As she walked back to the table, the server was bringing the food. She sat eating and didn't say much. Alphonso felt that neither of them could wait for the meal to be over.

She could at least be respectful. She hasn't spent any of her own money. He'd even bought the souvenirs she purchased with the cash Alphonso gave her, and when that ran out, they used Alphonso's credit card.

For a few minutes, they ate in silence, and he was happy about that; he'd just about had enough of her.

"My food is great. Some types of herbs in this boil give it a distinct taste that I haven't had before. How is yours?" asked Jocelyn, but her voice was stern, and the conversation was forced.

"No one makes gumbo as they do in Louisiana, but it's good. My crabs and shrimp are some of the bests I have had. The key lime pie will be the actual test when the server brings it. And here it is now. Man, does it look good? This is the best, and I could eat it every day."

"I believe you could, too."

"Let me finish this up, so we can leave when the server brings my credit card. How was the lemon sorbet?"

"It was okay. I have had better," Jocelyn said.

"I have my card back, and we can be on our way."

"What time would you like to get dinner this evening, Jocelyn? It's our last meal, so it would be nice to finish the vacation on a friendly note."

"I don't want to eat with you tonight, Alphonso. I am going to pack my things and just order room service. What time should I be ready for departure?"

Well, that certainly told him. He wondered how anybody could be so cold or bad-mannered. "Our flight leaves at 8:30 a.m. We can set off for the airport no later than 6:30 a.m. If I remember, it's about a forty-five-minute drive."

"I'll meet you in the restaurant at six a.m."

"Is everything okay?"

"Yes. I just think we should spend the last night alone." Jocelyn stated. She was ice cold with him.

"Did I upset you or make you mad?" he asked.

"No. Neither. I thought I would make some phone calls home and pack. You know, sometimes we all need some alone time. You don't have to suffocate me."

"I am not sure what the alone time is about when we are to be on vacation together. Am I that bad that I need to check myself?" he asked.

"Alphonso, I don't see the point in continuing this conversation. I'm going to my room now. I will see you in the morning and have a good night."

"You have a good night, as well."

Something happened that put her in this mood. It was suspicious, but Alphonso would not waste any time trying to figure it out. It was only four-thirty. He'd take a shower, look at some notes from the case, and make some phone calls—and then he was going to go out and enjoy his last evening. He would have cocktails at the bar and dinner in a pleasant restaurant with live music and dancing.

Chapter Twenty-Seven

FINALLY GOING HOME

Alphonso had a headache, and it told him he's out of practice hanging out and drinking. Vacations were about relaxing and doing things you don't do every day. Alphonso was glad that he'd packed his things last night. The state he's in, he didn't know if he could do it this morning. Once Alphonso ran through the shower, everything would be okay. He had to meet Jocelyn at 6 a.m., and it was 5:45 a.m. The room was spinning.

He's dressed, ready, and feeling better, but he wasn't looking forward to more awkwardness between him and Jocelyn. Her refusal to have dinner with him last night made the vacation even more dreadful.

Jocelyn was sitting in a booth next to the kitchen entrance. I guess that says it all. There would be no relationship between them, but it didn't stop her from looking like a beauty queen. He'd thought he was the sick one for putting up with the critical attitude from her.

"Good morning. How was your night?" Alphonso asked.

"Are you asking out of interest or in your role as an investigator?"

"My night was uneventful. Mia and I talked for an hour. I had room service for dinner and went to bed. I didn't meet up with any men. No excitement."

He'd tried to believe she's a wonderful mother to her daughter.

"Well, I ventured out to the hotel bar. I had dinner and some drinks. The hotel guests packed the place last night, and they had live music from some locals. They had karaoke, and I took part. It was a good night. You would've enjoyed it, I think. Are you ready for the long trip today?"

"Exactly, how long is it? I lost track of time coming here because of the time zones."

"It's twelve hours, and we'll go through three time zones before reaching Fairbanks. We should arrive around twelve or twelve-thirty Saturday morning. We've a fifty-minute layover in Atlanta, and we change planes there. But we've a five-hour layover in Seattle, and I checked our flights. Every connection is running on time."

"When we get to Atlanta, I'll phone my mother to let her know how late we'll be arriving."

"Their servers are friendly here. I would give customer service in the hotel an A." Alphonso noted.

"Alphonso their chain of this hotel was beautiful with lots of extras you don't get at other hotels, and the food was some of the best I'd had in a long time."

"From what you've said about it, I didn't think it impressed you. When do you go back to work?'

"On Monday. So, I'll have time to spend the weekend with my daughter and do some other things I've been putting off. How about you?"

"Tomorrow, I am going to rest. Sunday, I'll probably drive into the office and catch up on some emails, so they don't throw everything at me on Monday morning. I've missed being at work, but it's nice taking a break for a few days."

"I've had enough food, Alphonso, so whenever you're ready, I can get my things and meet you outside my door."

"Sounds like a plan. See you in five minutes."

He'd did a final walk-thru of his room to ensure he wasn't leaving anything. Alphonso was determined to find out why Jocelyn was making such a long-distance move to Hawaii and away from her mother. He's surprised by her business-like attitude at breakfast. He'd expected it to be her tempo for the entire trip back to Alaska. It suited him.

"I was about to call you, but you were already outside your door waiting for me."

"Do you have some loose change Alphonso, so I can leave a tip for housekeeping? I don't know if people do that these days. I'd always felt like they do a lot of cleaning up behind us and get meager wages for doing it."

"Yes. I didn't think of that. But if you give me a minute, I am going to leave one as well."

Walking in silence to the car, Alphonso had one last glance at the beach. The next time he'd visits, it would be with his wife.

"It's such a beautiful day after all the rain last night," Jocelyn said.

"I'm glad we're going to have pleasant weather for flying because traveling in the rain is no fun."

"The drive across the Gulf of Mexico bridge is stunning; it's a view I will never forget."

"It is spectacular. We're leaving early, Jocelyn, so with a bit of luck, the airport won't be crowded."

"Let's hope so. I don't feel like dealing with people today. I'm looking forward to seeing my daughter and mother. As I think about it, I miss work, too."

"Yes, we do all the planning and preparations to get away from the office, and while we're on vacation, people talk about work the most. I'm lucky and have a great team that holds the fort in my absence. Sometimes it scares me they do a better job than me." They both laughed.

"Well, I don't have that worry at Delta, but when I start my new job, it's something I will have to consider."

"I can drop you off at the departure entrance; then you don't have to wait for me to go through the headache of returning the car."

"No, I don't mind waiting while you check in the car. I need to do some walking. I've had little exercise since we got here. We have a small exercise room at home, and I get up early to exercise before dealing with my daughter in the mornings. She's not a morning person, and it's a job for me trying to get her ready for school. But I wouldn't have it any other way."

After the rental car company attendant finished the car's inspection, they went to get checked in at the Delta counter. As they hoped, the airport was almost empty of passengers. Getting their tickets and security walkthrough was a piece of cake.

"I'm going to stop at the bathroom and freshen up; we've some time before departure," Jocelyn said.

While in the restroom, she texted her friend because she didn't want anyone to hear her conversation with him. She had to distance herself as much as possible, and she did not want to get in a lengthy discussion. Her message to her friend was to implement their plan on Sunday instead of Monday. She'd learned from him that a new guy was working at the hotel. He'd been snooping around and asking the staff questions about the incident in Amelia's office. Shed told him there couldn't be any mistakes or traces back to either of them, or he's to call her once completed. Her friend wanted to know why he had to do all the dirty work. She'd told him he had the skills and would get paid a large sum of money, so he could return his family back home to Texas, and then she stopped texting after that statement.

She'd only had time left to text her mother about the expected arrival time on Saturday morning. She freshened her makeup and heard the Delta attendant calling for her flight to board. She was happy that they had first-class seating.

Walking behind Jocelyn down the narrow hallway to board the plane, he'd realized something was wrong with her. He'd never met somebody so self-obsessed and uncaring. Being in her presence was frightening."

They were silent on the trip from Pensacola to Atlanta Hartsfield-Jackson International airport, where they had to change planes. She's had what she wanted from him and had frozen him out.

With the second leg of their trip from Atlanta to Seattle-Tacoma International in Washington, they had a five-hour layover. It was 5:00 p.m. and dinner time. They agreed to eat at Qdoba Mexican restaurant. Alphonso felt like leaving her to starve, but he's too much of a gentleman.

Their orders arrived, and there was minimal conversation.

"I'm going to walk around and stop into some boutiques and other shops we passed since we've a significant wait time for our next flight."

"I will sit here and have another margarita or two. Do you need any money, or are you all right?"

"Well, I'd like to get a bottle of perfume, some sweets for Mia, and a nice scarf for Mom, if you don't mind." Alphonso sighed as he opened his wallet. She has some nerve—what a monster.

"Why don't we meet back at our departure gate? That way, we don't have to wonder where either of us is."

"That is a great idea. I'll see you then," Jocelyn said.

Alphonso sat in the restaurant for an hour after eating and had another margarita. Their last flight would depart at 9:20 p.m.

They were both at the gate in good time to board the plane to Fairbanks.

"While sitting at the gate, I heard the Delta attendant tell everyone waiting that the flight is only half full, and people can change seats if they like after take-off. I think I might like to have a seat on my own, Alphonso, so that I can stretch out."

"Fine. I noticed there weren't many passengers waiting at the gate."

"Yes, people don't enjoy flying at night. They want to see where they are going when the plane takes off," she replied.

"It doesn't matter to me when I fly, as long as I get there in one piece."

"I guess for me; it does because I don't get to fly that often. It would've been better if we'd paid more for daytime flights."

The flight attendant asked if they wanted a drink before takeoff, and they both declined. Within fifteen minutes, they were in the air.

"I noticed you had several bags, Jocelyn, so I guess the shopping was a success."

"I got the perfume I wanted and purchased several things for Mia, including some small toys. How was your wait time?"

"I didn't have to shop for anyone but come to think of it; I should've picked something up for the administrator at the office. Without her support, the office would be in trouble. But I just sat in the same restaurant we had dinner and had another margarita. Then I came back to the gate and did some reading."

"I didn't know how exhausting this trip was until the way back home. I will have no trouble falling asleep when my head hits the pillow. I'm going to change seats so that I can get some sleep before we land. I'm sure you understand."

"Perfectly," Alphonso said.

After they deplaned, they met at Alphonso's car, and Alphonso felt he should say something before they reached her house.

"I know the trip didn't turn out the way we hoped it would, so I want to say I'm sorry."

"Right now, a lot is going on with me, Alphonso, and I hope you will forgive me, too. Maybe someday we can get together as friends," Jocelyn said apologetically.

"Here we are. I'll wait until you are safe inside. You have a wonderful weekend with your family."

"Thank you, Alphonso, and you be safe driving home."

He arrived home and jumped into bed without unpacking.

Chapter Twenty-Eight

A TERRIBLE ACCIDENT

On Sunday morning, Alphonso headed to the office after resting for the day on Saturday. He couldn't wait to get back to work after a terrible vacation. Alphonso wasn't even excited about marking days on his soulmate calendar. He'd wanted to find out what had gone on in the past between Jason and Jocelyn. He had an idea but needed more evidence before confronting him on Monday morning. There would be no distractions because Alphonso was the only one going into the office.

Sometimes the truth hurts worse than lies. The first honest attempt to find a soulmate struck out, but Alphonso wouldn't give up. Sometimes you search for something, and you were so blind you couldn't see what was in front of you. Jocelyn was beautiful, but she wasn't a nice person, after all. He's glad they went away together, and he'd saw what she's really like before it was too late. He'd be more cautious about who he dates in the future.

Liam and his team had been working on this case and had uncovered additional evidence. They're on track for a resolution based on what they'd found and what he'd learned in Pensacola.

He'd finished his breakfast and headed to the office. The sooner he got there, the sooner he could return home.

Alphonso had driven the Scenic View Highway every day since he'd became an employee of Soco. He never realized how steep the cliff on the highway's right side was until now. It's a dangerous road if you travel at high speed, but he's a careful driver. Alphonso put some music on the radio. The second he'd turned away from the road, a car came from nowhere on the left side. It was traveling at high speed and hit the left side of his car. Before he could react, his car careened over the cliff, and all he could think about was he hadn't had time to get married.

It's a quiet Sunday morning, and an hour passed before another car came down the highway and saw smoke as he'd approached the cliff where Alphonso's vehicle went over. The driver called 911, and within minutes, police, ambulance, and the fire department were onsite. More personnel and the news media arrived soon after. It's four hours before they pulled the body from the car and two more hours to pull the car up the cliff. They searched for identification. The person in the vehicle was Alphonso Lott. He's barely breathing and was unconscious.

Jason hated doing paperwork. He's sitting in his office at home finishing up a document for Joan to format on Monday morning. A breaking news report came on the TV. There had been a terrible accident on the Scenic View Highway. That highway's name was familiar to him. He'd realized it was the one that Alphonso traveled to work on. They flashed pictures of a car they'd recovered, and he'd recognized it as Alphonso's 1947 Mercedes. The one his father gave him.

"Oh my God. That can't be Alphonso; he just got home from vacation," Jason says out loud.

The news said that one victim, a male, was in the car and taken to the local hospital. He ran to tell his wife and let her know he's going to the hospital. He'd hoped Alphonso's parents hadn't seen the news. He would call Alphonso's sister when he got to the hospital.

As he walked into the emergency waiting room, Alphonso's entire family were there, including his parents. Through very teary eyes, his sister thanked Jason for coming and said that Alphonso was alive but in a coma. His injuries were so severe that the doctor didn't know how he survived the accident. Alphonso's parents were hanging in there and doing okay. Still, he'd saw his sister wasn't handling it very well and was crying uncontrollably. Jason offered to help her husband comfort her.

The police officer told them his car pushed over the cliff and hit a tree. That's what had saved him; otherwise, his vehicle would have fallen to the bottom of the cliff. Jason tried to comfort the family. He'd got coffee from the vending machine and called his wife, then Jermaine. Next, he rang Liam and Joan to update them on Alphonso's condition.

He'd hoped they'd heard some good news soon. After three hours, the doctor said there was no change in his condition and that he's still in a coma and his condition critical. His brain had some function, but they had him on a ventilator, and the next six hours were going to be crucial for his survival.

Jason decided there was nothing he could do, so he went home. Alphonso had a close family support system. Whatever he needed, if he survived, they would be there for him.

Back at home, he'd gave his wife an update on Alphonso's condition. His wife didn't work, and he asked her to keep the children at home on Monday. He didn't want to frighten her, but he'd said it was just a precaution when she wondered why. He'd asked his brother to do the same with his wife and kids.

Who could've done this to Alphonso? He'd worked on many cases over the years, and nobody had ever tried to kill him. It must be tied to the case he'd been working. If so, it could mean that the entire firm, and even Amelia, may be in danger. He would make calls to the firm staff, Amelia, and the Anchorage police chief. So, from his home office, Jason sent out an emergency text to his entire team to call in. He was calling an office conference number within ten minutes to speak to them all at once. They'd all seen the news and called before the time he requested.

Jason informed them what had happened to Alphonso. He'd told them where Alphonso was in the hospital, his condition and everything the doctor had relayed to him and Alphonso family. Jason advised on the state of Alphonso's family and how critical it was going to be over the next few hours. He explained that he'd wanted everyone to be cautious and careful the next twenty-four hours because their lives could be in danger. He didn't want them to be surprised. Jason did not have any specific evidence to back this claim, except it was just instinct and what the police had reported.

A vehicle intentionally pushed Alphonso's car over the cliff. He believed that it all related to Amelia's case. Jason realized the team did not know Jocelyn, but she was on vacation with Alphonso. From the last conversation they had, he'd felt it involved her in their case. He wanted everyone at work on Monday because this is what Alphonso would like them to do. Jason let Joan know he would pick her up at 8:30 a.m. because he didn't want her driving alone.

"Hello, Amelia, this is Jason. I know it is late, and I apologize. Alphonso's had an attempt on his life this afternoon, and we think it's related to your case. However, I don't want you to panic because we're not positive. I just want you to take extra precautions. He's at Fairbanks Memorial Hospital, and his condition is critical. The doctors will update his family on his condition tomorrow. I am calling you because we want you to watch your surroundings and be aware of anything suspicious. We have contacted our guy onsite, so he's watching out for anything out of the ordinary."

"Thank you so much. I hope everything will be okay with Alphonso. Please keep me updated on his condition. He's incredibly special to me."

"I will. You have a good night."

"Goodnight."

Jason wanted to cuddle his wife and kids and have time to process the information himself. But he had to make sure everybody was informed.

His last call was to the Chief in Anchorage. He told the Chief of his suspicions and connections between Anchorage and an attempted murder case of Alphonso in Fairbanks. The Chief agreed with an assessment based on the conversation he had with the police chief in Fairbanks earlier.

After speaking with his brother, Liam, Noah, Joan, James, Amelia, and the Chief of Police, Jason felt better that they were aware of his concerns. If Jocelyn was involved in this, he didn't know what her motivation was. He felt guilty because he tried to warn Alphonso about dating her. He'd wished he had interfered and told him to stay the hell away from her. It was a rough night for all, but he tried to get some sleep.

Chapter Twenty-Nine

IT'S NOT OVER

Jocelyn wasn't ready to face the Delta passengers this Monday morning. Walking to her work area, she took a call from an unknown number. She thought it was the call she should've received last night.

"Hello Jocelyn, this is Tyler, your favorite person in the world."

"You are no one's favorite, not even your wife. What do you want this early in the morning?"

"Leave my wife out of this. Why didn't you call me while you were in Pensacola?"

"I did, but you didn't answer your phone."

"I was sick for a few days with a virus. William told me you were here, with some investigator guy from a Fairbanks law firm. He's concerned about you. And then this morning, I see the same guy he's telling me about was in a terrible accident last night and is in a coma. The news report says it was not an accident. What the hell is going on? I thought you were working on a deal with me. But it seems like you've got your own deal going on. Or am I being paranoid?"

"Why would you think I'm involved in this?"

"Because I know your history with my brother. You'll do anything to get what you want, and you'll take care of anyone or anything that gets in the path of your objectives. What's this? I hear about an investigator working at Amelia's hotel. You'd better not mess this deal up for me.

Many people's lives are affected if we don't pull it off—including yours." Tyler's threat was open and unveiled.

"Is there something going on with our deal that I don't know?" Tyler asked.

"No. You know everything you need to. How did you know about the investigator staying at the hotel?"

"If you plan on moving to Hawaii, you'd better stick to the original plan and find out about this guy at the hotel."

"We're on track."

"If I find out you're involved in this accident with the investigator, you can forget about Hawaii. You have a nice day."

Jocelyn didn't understand why Evan didn't call last night. He should've updated her by now. Jocelyn had one more thing to do, and the task would be complete. She thought they should wait until things smoothed over with Alphonso. He should be dead. What went wrong? She and Mia would be in Hawaii before the investigation into his attack started.

Chapter Thirty

HOW MANY INVOLVED

After Jason had a long night, he was up early to pick up Joan at her home.

"Good morning Joan, how was the rest of your night?"

"Thanks for picking me up this morning. I couldn't sleep a wink, knowing that someone tried to take Alphonso's life. Being in the office will help me keep my mind focused."

"Yes, being here is the best for all of us. Alphonso is like a brother to me, and I don't know what I'll do if he doesn't survive. Alphonso the investigator, with a second name stubborn. He'll not let this beat him. Joan, I've not met with his team, but at 11 a.m. I'd like to. Please have everyone gathered in conference room. As much as we'd like to be at the hospital, he'd want us to continue working this case concerning Amelia."

"I would need you to take notes and I'd planned on going to the hospital around 1:00 p.m. Could you come with me and I'll drop you at home after we've left the hospital if that's okay."

"Yes, I'd like to see him and speak with his family."

"Jason, I can't forget the last conversation I had with Alphonso out of my mind. He'd been so excited about his upcoming vacation."

" Joan, I feel you, but I have to make some phone calls"

Jason called the Fairbanks police station to speak to the Chief of police working Alphonso's case. Acting as Alphonso's lawyer, he'd asked for an update. The Chief confirmed it had been a deliberate murder attempt.

He noted a hidden camera was on the highway Alphonso traveled that day and whoever did this, probably planned it before cameras was recently installed.

They'd identified the car from the camera. The license plate recorded it as a rental car, and the customer paid with cash and used a false name. Police department had put out a public news request with a reward for anybody on the road that may have seen something.

Jason thanked him for the update.

Jason wondered how this incident, Amelia's case, and the threat messages on his phone related. He spoke aloud, "Jocelyn."

Jason had an affair with her before her husband's death. To add to his list of immoral and unprofessional crimes, he'd represented her at trial as her counsel. He'd defended her during the case involving her husband's death. They'd found her not guilty, and they'd decreed the death was an accident. She'd wanted to resume their affair after he'd died, but he had not agreed to it. It left her bitter and vengeful. After telling his wife and almost ending their marriage didn't get him back, she'd resorted to threats as the woman scorned.

Alphonso had one date and went on a week's vacation with her. William, Amelia's brother, met with her in Pensacola. There were too many circles and connections, and they'll linked back to Jocelyn. Jason felt that she's punishing him for breaking off the relationship. If she's doing all this to hurt him, she's a dangerous person, and who would she try to break next. Joan came in to tell him that Alphonso's team was in the conference room.

"Time goes by fast." They all agreed in unison.

"I called this meeting to see where we're at with Amelia's case."

"Alphonso had sent us his notes before leaving Pensacola. Their concerns about Amelia's brother, the information Tyler's wife gave him, and the actions of the police at Amelia's hotel regarding one of her staff members. We think there're more than two people involved in this case," Liam explained.

"What evidence brings you to that conclusion?" Jason asked.

"Someone wanted this hotel bad, and whoever that is, has planned how they're going to take it from Amelia. This person isn't doing the dirty work; they've hired someone to carry it out. Their must be somebody familiar with the hotel that they trust. Alphonso's accident may be part of their scheme."

"Who do you think they are?"

"Based on Alphonso's findings, William and Jocelyn are two of the most likely people involved. We don't have enough intel to know who else may be a part of this plot yet. They tried to kill two people; the perpetrator is somebody ruthless, desperate, or both. They'll have a partner."

"It's ironic that you name Jocelyn because I thought she may be involved. I suspect the police in Anchorage as well. Where do we go from here?"

"Anchorage Chief of police has to be given a heads up by you, Jason, since this firm is representing Amelia."

"I agree. After speaking with Fairbanks Chief of Police regarding Alphonso's case, they've a suspect car, but not a suspect." Jason filled them in on what the Chief told him. "Alphonso has police guarding him outside his door because they don't know if this person will come back to finish him."

"Joan and I are going to see him after this meeting. We've had word from the family that any of us can go see him anytime. If the family had any request of this office, that takes precedence over everything else. It looks like we're on track, and I believe this case will end soon. We'll continue to pray that Alphonso makes a full recovery. Noah is taking Amelia to see him tomorrow."

"Alphonso shared with me that he'd had a relationship with Amelia when they were in high school, but no other details. She was distraught on the phone and cares about him very much. We need to be sensitive to her feelings. So, let's do whatever we need to ensure she has a safe visit to see him and a safe journey back to the hotel. Thank you all for the update, and let's move swiftly to get a resolution. Joan and I'll go home after we visit Alphonso, so we'll see you tomorrow."

Chapter Thirty-One

EVERYTHING IN JEOPARDY

Tyler didn't want his wife to know they were in financial trouble and on the verge of losing everything. That included their company, the house, and all the real estate properties he'd inherited from his father. His lawyer had drawn up bankruptcy papers. He'd said it was time to disclose a restriction clause in the will that only his father and Cadence, his wife, knew about. If the company was near bankruptcy, Cadence would become the CEO, and Tyler could no longer work in any decision-making role for the company.

With the weight of this on his shoulders, he'd went about day-to-day living as if nothing was wrong. Once he'd discovered how serious the mess was, he'd knew the loan with Lawdale Financial Group to construct Tyler's project would be due right away. Especially if his agreement to purchase failed. His failure would be because of the trust he'd placed in two amateurs, Jocelyn, and her associate. He'd put so much faith into that woman that he didn't argue when she refused to divulge her associate's name to him. He'd been a fool.

He'd wondered how Jocelyn got mixed up with Alphonso, the enemy. Tyler knew she's familiar with Jason at Soco & Soco, but he thought that was in the past. Had Jocelyn doubled-crossed him and gone rogue with Jason on another deal? She could get more money than he'd offered. He'd seen the news about Alphonso being in an accident. Tyler needed answers today from his buddy Connor at the police department in Anchorage. The house of cards was tottering and threatening to fall.

"Hello, Connor, don't say my name. I need some clarification from you today, or my family is going to be homeless."

"What are you talking about?"

"There's a guy at Amelia's hotel snooping around and asking the staff questions. Are you aware of him, and who is he working for?"

"Yes, I know who he is and why he's here. He works for Soco & Soco on Alphonso's team of investigators. He's been at the hotel for a couple of days as an additional security detail for Amelia."

"Does that mean she's hired a lawyer? How close are they to finding out what we are doing?" Tyler asked, and he couldn't mask the panic building in his voice.

"As of Friday, last week, they don't know who's involved in the threats to Amelia."

"We've one thing to do, and I can't trust Jocelyn to do it. So, I'm counting on you, Connor. When can you do it, and can I count on you to complete?"

"I'll do it tomorrow, but we have to be careful because of the attack on Alphonso."

"Yes, I know. In the meantime, I'm preparing for the worst. Talk to you later." Connor hung up and put his head in his hands.

Chapter Thirty-Two

THE LAST THREAT

Amelia was reminiscing and couldn't explain the emptiness in her heart until the day she walked into the Soco & Soco law firm's conference room. To her surprise, Alphonso was sitting at the table. It was hard for her to contain herself, and her heart felt like it was going to jump out of her chest. During the afternoon of the same day, while she was back at her parent's vacation home in Fairbanks, he'd called her, and this time she was surprised but better prepared.

Alphonso was in a coma at Fairbanks memorial hospital, fighting for his life. Would she have time to tell him how she felt or was it too late? She couldn't rest until she saw him.

Shoving aside warnings about her safety, she'd make the trip to see him. She wanted to go right away, but there was no relief manager to take over from her, and she couldn't leave the hotel. Again, the business she loved could cause her to lose the man she'd loved. While signing invoices for payment of services at the hotel, her phone rang.

"Hello, Hotel International-Anchorage, Amelia speaking, how can I help you?"

A mean male voice said, "This is your last chance to sell the hotel before something happens to your brother and your hotel staff. You have twenty-four hours to decide."

Shaken after the phone call, she'd sat at her desk, not knowing what to do. Her first instinct was to call her brother, the police, and Jason in that order. There's so much speculation about who could be involved that she didn't trust anybody. She'd trust Alphonso if she could talk to him. Did she need to warn her staff, and how would she do that? She'd rang for Noah and requested he came to her office to advise her.

Noah was with her in minutes, and they had Jason on speakerphone explaining. "Amelia, I need you to contact the police and let them inform your employees about the danger. Noah will not leave your side until the police instruct the next step. I'll call your brother and make him aware of the threat." Jason was in control and told them what to do.

"Jason, have you heard any news about Alphonso?"

"I spoke to his sister this morning; she stayed at the hospital overnight. There's no change in his condition."

"Thank you for the update, but I must see him. I can't leave until tomorrow, but can Noah drive me there first thing, please?"

"Amelia, after the phone call today, you could put yourself in further danger."

"I know it's not a good idea, but I'm going with or without Noah. There's something I need to say to him, and I'd have to say it in person. I will stay overnight at my vacation home, and there's enough room for Noah if he doesn't mind. I'm sorry for the inconvenience, Jason, but I'm going to do this."

"Since you insist. Make the police aware of your intentions when they arrive. They may give you a police escort. Noah, call me later to update."

"Okay, Jason. Thank you for everything," Amelia said.

After their conversation and taking instructions from the police, Amelia and Noah went to their rooms to pack an overnight bag. During her trip, one of the police officers assigned to a 30-day detail at the hotel would follow her and Noah at a distance, and they'd stay outside her house on Tuesday night. She'd felt better knowing that she would get to see Alphonso and that the police escort would be nearby.

Chapter Thirty-Three

WHY ME WHY NOW

Amelia didn't sleep all night because she couldn't stop thinking about Alphonso. She had breakfast brought to her room and afterwards got dressed for her trip. Amelia knew the drive would be a long one because she'd made this trip so many times to Fairbanks. She was glad Noah was driving because she would not be able to go it alone at this point. Amelia slept most of the way to Fairbanks, and there was minimal conversation between them. She and Noah arrived at the hospital in time to meet Alphonso's family, and it was an emotional reunion.

Amelia was surprised at the warm greeting she'd received from Alphonso's family; they all remembered her. And they told her that Alphonso had mentioned they were back in touch. There were no objections to her seeing Alphonso. Their reaction validated her reason for being there. She'd went into his room escorted by Noah, who only stayed five minutes before giving them their privacy. He'd took up a formidable stance outside the hospital room door. After the police let her in, she didn't know what to say to him.

Alphonso had bruises and deep lacerations all over his face and arms, but he'd looked as though he's in a peaceful sleep. She'd stood by his bedside with tears in her eyes and put his hand in hers.

"Alphonso, this is Amelia, and it's okay if you can't hear me. I'm here, and I'd hope you can feel that. I've been so worried about you.

There are things I need to say, but I don't know how to express them. You've a wonderful family, and evidently, you've said some nice things about me to them because they greeted me so warmly. You're what has been missing in my life all these years. I didn't want to admit it. My heart is aching, seeing you in such a state and knowing you can't respond. I have to say all this now because I don't know if I would dare say it if you were awake. I blame my parents for insisting that I'd learn the hotel business and making me miss out on a life of love with you. Alphonso, I've loved you since high school. Men have approached me over the years, but my heart belongs to you. It would help if you fought this coma like you and I used to hit the gym in high school. I'd want you to fight Alphonso—do it for us. I'm going to wait for you, no matter how long it takes. The last thing you said to me in high school was, 'Why me. Why now.' Those same words are in my mouth today. I can't lose you again. My time is up because your doctor would only let me in for fifteen minutes. But I'll see you soon."

Amelia placed his hand back on the bed. She reached down and kissed him on the lips and walked out with tears in her eyes. As she got to the waiting room, she'd wiped her tears away.

She thanked his family for allowing her to spend time with him and said she'd pray for him to be whole again.

Chapter Thirty-Four

FACTS COME TOGETHER

Puzzled and sad by what happened to Alphonso, Jason was at home in his office after he and Joan visited him in the hospital. The doctor said there was still no change, and there might not be for weeks. Jason was thinking about going to bed, but his phone rang, interrupted his thoughts.

"Hello?"

"Jason, this is the Chief of Police Archey from Anchorage. I have been in contact with Fairbanks' Chief of Police Farley. We discussed this Jocelyn Sandy character and her encounter with Amelia Haley brother in Pensacola last week. With the additional information you provided and the timing of the accident, we believe they're tied together."

"Can you give me a little more than that?"

"From the start of this case and the first conversation I had with you, I've been watching my two officers assigned to the case. We've had suspicions about one of them and have had one under covert surveillance for several months. His actions concerning another case raised suspicion. However, that's all it was, some erratic behavior, and we've had no evidence to charge him with anything, or even enough to take him off the job. Then we placed a tracker on his phone because we were still concerned. The calls from his phone have been coming from numbers in Alaska and Pensacola. We know the person he's in cahoots with in Pensacola and have alerted the police there with our arrest plan and transport of that person to Alaska."

"There are multiple people involved in Alaska. I'd traced the predominant number in question to Jocelyn Sandy. We believe that she's connected to the accident, but we know she didn't cause it herself. The Chief in Fairbanks received an anonymous call concerning the vehicle that hit Alphonso, and he's validating that information. Until we're sure of all the evidence and can confirm our sources, this is strictly confidential and the most I can tell you."

"This is great. I was wondering when there was going to be a break in either case. I guess this is it. Excellent work, Chief Archey. Is Amelia's brother involved?"

"No, he's not, and he's the least of our worries. I'd just wanted to give you a heads up since Amelia Haley is your client."

"Thank you for the information. I'll let my staff know what you've uncovered, and if it's okay, I'll give Amelia a heads up to remain cautious."

"That will be fine. Just don't give Amelia any details. You have a good evening."

"Thank you, and you do the same."

Jason placed a call to Liam, gave them the good news, and then rang Amelia. Sometime this week, the case would be over, and everybody could concentrate on helping Alphonso.

Chapter Thirty-Five

ALL THE ARRESTS

At ten o'clock on Wednesday night, the police were ready to swoop. The Anchorage and Fairbanks police departments had liaised regarding Alphonso's accident and Amelia's threat case. They'd gathered enough evidence for arrests.

At eleven-thirty p.m., they arrested Evan Shaw at his home. At the same time, Jocelyn Sandy, one of Delta airline's attendants, was taken into custody. Simultaneously, in Florida, Tyler Small of Hailer, LLC was arrested. Tyler Small would be transferred to the Anchorage police department on Friday morning. Each of them was interrogated and booked on several charges relating to both crimes. To retrieve supporting evidence, the suspect's homes and businesses were searched. Officers recovered cell phones, burner phones, laptops, iPads, and a multitude of incriminating documents.

They were allowed to notify their lawyers.

On Wednesday afternoon, before leaving work, Jason and his brother gave all the staff Thursday and Friday off because they were concerned about Alphonso. Jason understood their pain because he'd felt it, too. After getting home, having dinner with his family, and putting their children to bed, he and his wife were up late streaming a movie—the phone rang.

"Hello, this is Jason?"

"Jason, sorry to call you so late. This is Chief Archey from the Anchorage police department. I have some great news."

"Can you go somewhere private so we can talk?"

"Yes, please continue."

"The Chief Farley and I agreed this evening that we've enough evidence to make arrests in the accident involving Alphonso and the threats against Amelia. There is some additional information involving four threat messages to your cell phone that came to light. You failed to inform us about those, and it could have impeded the investigation. By right, we should arrest you for withholding evidence. Given the delicate nature of the situation, I'll do what I can to bury it. Enough people have already been hurt, don't you think?"

"Thank you. I appreciate that."

"We arrested Evan Shaw, an employee of Amelia's at his home, for the attempted murder of Alphonso by running him off the road. He did it for Jocelyn Sandy because Alphonso stood in the way of a big payout by investigating Amelia's threats. And, as a separate favor to Jocelyn, because she's trying to destroy you, your firm, and your family. Jocelyn has coughed and admitted everything. She claims your affair resulted in her becoming pregnant with your daughter. She says you've denied being the father. Is that true?"

"I had an affair with her, but she was already pregnant by her husband before getting together with me. While she was in Pensacola on vacation with Alphonso, I had a DNA test done. Her mother called me because she knew about the affair and suspected I was not Mia's father. We all needed to know the truth. It's been a secret for too long—and secrets destroy families. It turns out I'm not the father. Alphonso wasn't aware of my affair, but I'd intended to tell him everything when he returned from his vacation. I felt he was making a mistake dating her. I wished I'd told him sooner."

"I'm glad you cleared that up because it could have been a problem when she goes to trial. She's the one sending the threat texts to your phone from a burner. We found out that she and Evan worked on a contract for hire from Tyler Small of Hailer, LLC real-estate developers in Florida. Their job was to work together with the threats to Amelia's phone, her emails, postal mail, and her office for monetary gain. The one thing Tyler told no one was the underlying reason for this entire crime. Amelia's grandparents saved his grandparents from bankruptcy by purchasing the land from them where the hotel sits today. He'd wanted to avenge his grandparents by getting that land back."

"Because of that, Tyler is about to lose his business, his home, and additional real-estate his father gained before he died in bankruptcy. His father made a separate will that Tyler found out about that had some conditions and stipulations to transfer the business into his wife's name if he got the business into trouble. This was when he tried to get William to convince his sister to sell the hotel, but the deal fell through. William didn't know that Tyler forced his hand and tried to threaten his sister into selling after their deal failed. Tyler made a deal with a friend of his at Lawdale Financial Group to loan him money until this hit went through with Amelia. Tyler is in default to Lawdale Financial Group for a large sum of money."

"I see. Thank you for letting me know all this," Jason said.

"The part that burns me about this mess is Tyler got my officer Connor Wynn involved. He's a good cop. Connor was going in behind Evan and Jocelyn and making threats via the phone. Connor hid evidence from the other officers. He was protecting Evan. He's helped Tyler with some other shady deals because Tyler stopped Connor from losing his home several years ago. Connor Wynn was arrested, as well."

"The innocent person who's been hurt and may not survive is Alphonso. I've little sympathy for a police officer that's had his head turned by a civilian," Jason said.

"Have there been any changes in Alphonso's condition?"

"Not yet, but he has a noble family who will help him through this. I think he'll have support from Amelia, too. She was his high school sweetheart and never fell out of love with him. Of course, he's not aware of it because she didn't tell him before the accident. Some good has to come out of all this."

"After Connor Wynn's arrest, we've scheduled a press conference for Friday."

"One more shot in the arm. Tyler was also in the process of purchasing all the condos in Alphonso's community to make it a live work and play, like the plans for Anchorage hotel. Of course, that's fallen through as well."

"I don't think Alphonso was aware of that because none of us knew." Jason was surprised.

"I'll inform my staff, Amelia, and Alphonso's family what has happened in the morning since it won't be on the news until Friday. This good news will take a weight off the shoulders of many people, especially my staff. It's going to break up relationships and cause some heartaches, too. Thank you for doing such good police work."

"We do our best. Goodnight, Jason."

"Goodnight, Chief Archey."

Chapter Thirty-Six

RECOVERY BEGINS

Jason was up early to call his brother, their staff, Amelia, and Alphonso's family. He'd felt a weight lifted off his shoulders. He had woken with hope in his heart, a far cry from the morning after Alphonso's tragic accident four days ago. Now they just needed Alphonso to wake up. Even though he'd had good news from the police and felt better, he wasn't going to the office because he'd be the only one there. He and his wife were going to visit Alphonso, hoping there was some change.

When he'd spoke to Amelia on the phone, she was already at the hospital with Alphonso's family. Amelia sounded heartbroken. According to Noah's report, after they returned to Anchorage on Wednesday, he couldn't comfort her. She left Anchorage again on Wednesday evening without telling Noah or any of her staff at the hotel. It was genuine love.

Jason and his wife arrived at the hospital, and he was very emotional. Alphonso's family, Amelia, Joan, and Alphonso's team were all sitting together, hoping for a miracle. It was very humbling. As soon as he and his wife sat down, the doctor came out and gave them all the good news. Alphonso was waking up. They didn't know how his memory would be affected—but he'd asked to see Amelia. He kept mumbling, 'Why me. Why now.'

Only he and Amelia knew what this meant.

Note: From The Author

There are many book clubs on Social Media, but some have just started and are not sure what questions they should discuss during their meetings. I have added some suggested questions. The questions will also help you decide how much you enjoyed the book.

Wherever you have purchased your copy, please leave a review, and send a comment to my website at www.barbaramo08.com.

BARBARA MOSTELLA published her first fictional novel titled *Who Would Have Thought* in March 2019 and has published a sequel titled *Consequences of Crime, Greed, & Love*.

Available for purchase

The next book, titled *Don't Go There*, will be out soon.

CONSEQUENCES OF CRIME, GREED, & LOVE

Discussion Questions

1. Was the story unique or original?

    __Yes __No

2. Did the title suit the novel?

    __Yes __No

3. Who was the principal character?

    ____

4. Identify one location where the story takes place?

    ____

5. Did the principal character have an objective?

    ______Yes ______No

6. What day of the week did the story begin?

    ____

7. How was the pace of the book?

    ______Fast ______Too slow ______Just Right

8. Who was the victim in the story?

    ____

Author Bio

Barbara Mostella journeyed from her birthplace in Ashville, Alabama with all the tools to exceed from her deceased loving parents. First obtaining a Bachelor of Science degree from Alabama A & M University in Huntsville, Alabama. To a successful career with the department of Defense that ended in retirement at Ft. McPherson in Georgia. And now a fiction author living in Georgia with her husband James. She enjoys reading, writing, spending time with family, quilting when time permits, and line dancing with friends.

My motto: "Don't let anyone set the tone for your day except you and God."

www.ingramcontent.com/pod-product-compliance
Lightning Source LLC
Chambersburg PA
CBHW021157110726
47900CB00002B/621